GONERS

Jan-Andrew Henderson

Black Hart Entertainment

Edinburgh. Brisbane

First published 2019 by Black Hart

Black Hart Entertainment.
32 Glencoul Ave, Dalgetty Bay, Fife KY11 9XL.
Janandrewhenderson.com

Cover by Jan-Andrew Henderson.

Book Layout © 2017 BookDesignTemplates.com.
Cover by Panagiotis Lampridis (BookDesignStars).

Goners.
ISBN-978-1-64570-603-8 (Print)
ISBN-978-1-64570-604-5 (eBook)

Part 1

We humans have linked our destinies with our machines. Our technology has gotten so complex that we no longer can understand it or fully control it.

Danny Hillis. *Scientific American Magazine*

-1-

I try not to take things too seriously. You never know what dangers the island will throw your way, so why not live in the moment?

At this moment I was hanging by my fingertips, fifty feet above an ocean churning with Humble-Squid. It's hard not to take *that* seriously.

There was no point cursing my own stupidity. Or dwelling on the fact that a Humble-Squid is a living torpedo with eight tentacles ringing a mouth full of razors. Or remembering the occasion I saw one reach out of the water and tear a man's arm off.

I had to blank all that from my mind and concentrate on surviving.

"I can't believe I was this dumb!" I screamed, glancing down at the thrashing swells. "Look at the teeth on those things! My God, they're going to rip me limb from limb!"

The boy I'd been pursuing sat a few feet away, watching. A scrawny sort, with short sandy hair, a thin-lipped mouth and shifty eyes. He was a deserter – or Goner, as we Regulators call them – and he definitely had the upper hand now.

Four times, I'd hauled myself up and got a leg across the strut of the fishing rig I had slipped from. Each time, he sidled dispassionately over and kicked it off again. Now I no longer had the strength to try.

But I wasn't going to give my enemy the satisfaction of grovelling.

"Please, *please* don't let me die!" I pleaded. "I'll do anything!"

"You think I like this?" the Goner snapped. "It's tearing me apart!"

"Yeah, but not *literally*." I looked down again. "I'm going to be human confetti in a minute."

The boy followed my gaze and winced at the writhing tentacles.

"All right," he said reluctantly. "I'll help… if you promise to stop chasing me."

"My word is my bond," I panted. "I absolutely promise to stop chasing you."

"I don't believe it." The Goner was perspiring heavily, whether from fear or exertion, I couldn't tell. Didn't really seem important at that moment.

"I'm not exactly in a position to cross my heart," I added urgently.

My left hand slid off the strut and I gave a squawk of terror, reaching desperately up and grabbing the bar again. I only had a few seconds before my own weight pulled me into the abyss.

With a resigned sigh, the boy shuffled over and grabbed my wrists. I could feel the heat of his sweaty hands against my skin as he planted both feet wide apart and hauled with all his might.

Inch by inch, I was dragged away from the brink. When most of my torso was back on the fishing platform, I swung my legs up and rolled onto the weather-beaten wood. The Goner sat down heavily, massaging his arms. Although he was almost my height, he must have been twenty kilos lighter and was shaking with the effort of lifting me.

"Thank you," I said, gratefully. I admit, I was somewhat taken aback. All he had to do was let me fall and he would have gotten away.

People are weird sometimes. Or perhaps he genuinely believed me.

Moron.

"I appreciate what you did just now." I unfastened the stun baton from my belt. "But you're under arrest."

"You gave your word." The boy's eyes widened.

"I was hanging from a bit of scaffolding," I replied scornfully. "What did you expect me to say? *No deal kid, I'd rather be lunch?*"

"I live in hope." He spat on the ground in disgust.

"It's nothing personal." I pointed the weapon at his chest. "I'm a Regulator. This is what I do."

I didn't see how he could argue with that. He was a Goner and Regulators catch Goners. It's part of the job. All right, it didn't seem fair, the kid having just stopped me from becoming squid nibbles. But that's life on New Hebrides.

Still, I felt bad. So I did something really dumb.

"Tell you what." I reluctantly lowered the baton. "I'll count to twenty before I come after you. That's more of a chance than any other Regulator would offer."

The boy hesitated, ready to argue for more clemency. Then he looked into my eyes and gave up. Scrambling to his feet, he began to shimmy down the scaffolding of the fishing rig. By the time I stopped counting, he was on the ground and vanishing behind one of the processing huts.

I climbed down the way he had come, copying his route but moving more cautiously. The brush with death had made me wary and I hated myself for feeling so vulnerable. No. I hated *him* for making me feel so vulnerable.

Reaching the deck, I sprinted after my quarry. The Goner had a pretty good head start, but I'm fast and I've got stamina. If I could just keep him in sight, I knew I'd eventually catch up. If I'd thought otherwise, I wouldn't have given him a chance.

The boy knew it too. When I rounded the corner, he was halfway up the next fishing rig, squirming through the metal struts like a grub worming its way into an apple. The sun was directly above, turning him into an animated silhouette.

What the hell was he playing at? This was the last scaffolding on the row. A dead end. I'd chased him up one rig and almost died for my trouble, which was probably what he'd been banking on.

All right, he'd rescued me in the end. But he wasn't likely to do *that* again.

Like my quarry, I had no intention of making the same mistake twice. All I had to do was wait for the fugitive to come down, and he'd be in my custody. The boy squinted back at me and I resisted the temptation to wave. Didn't seem appropriate.

Suddenly the Goner stopped and pulled off his shirt.

Huh? Surely he wasn't going to dive into the ocean? He'd be eaten in seconds.

Then I saw it. One thin support wire, right above him, leading from this rig to a stout metal pin on the next pier.

Ooooh. Very clever. And bad news for me.

The boy looped his jacket over the cable and prepared to launch himself into the air. I mentally judged the distance from this dock to the next and quickly concluded it was too far for me to jump. Once the Goner reached the ground, I'd never get to him before he disappeared into the narrow alleyways of the fishing district.

I slid to a halt on the slippery concrete, sending up a salty spray.

That was the answer. Everything in the fishing area is wet.

The boy clutched both sides of his jacket, lifted his legs and glided towards sanctuary. I raced to the end of the pier, setting my baton to maximum charge. I jerked my arm back and threw it as hard as I could.

The Goner smashed into the deck of the next pier, rolling through a puddle of water and vaulting upright, at the same time as the stunner landed. It was several yards short of him, despite my best efforts. But close enough.

For a few seconds he stood, rooted to the spot, as the electrical charge from my weapon coursed through the shallow pool swallowing his feet.

Then he toppled over.

-2-

It took ten minutes to get to my quarry but he wasn't going anywhere in a hurry. In fact, he was just coming round as I reached him.

"That was a good effort, Goner," I said generously, handcuffing him. "For a moment, I thought you were going to escape."

"And you almost let me." There was no disguising the vehemence in the boy's voice. "I'll make sure the Town Council knows all about *that*."

My heart leapt. Giving my quarry a chance was a spur-of-the-moment decision but very dangerous. You don't break *any* rules around here. It's… a rule.

Honestly. You try to be nice and where does it get you?

"Nobody saw," I said defensively, glancing around to make certain. "Nobody will believe you."

"Probably not," the Goner admitted. "But you still disobeyed orders. It's the first step on a slippery slope." He gave a mirthless chuckle. "It's how *I* started."

"I assure you there's no chance of *me* ever deserting the island." I snorted. "I have a shiny baton, better rations than most and the coolest job on New Hebrides."

"And a conscience, though it's well hidden." The boy rolled onto his back and glared at me. "Are you really going to hand me over to be executed after I risked my life to pull you up? Nobody would know if you let me get away."

"Remember what you were saying about that slippery slope?" I pulled the troublemaker to his feet. "Anyway, I didn't ask for your help."

"Actually, you begged for it."

I couldn't argue with that.

"Jeez. Why did you become a Goner, anyhow?" I quickly changed the subject. "Why throw away your life?"

"Because I'm a curious sort. I began to question things."

"Question what things?"

"Oh my." The boy's eyes lit up. "You really *are* doomed."

At that point, I should have hit him on the head. Discussion over. But I was most definitely having an off day. Instead, I sat him on a mooring bollard and plonked myself opposite. I guess I felt obliged to allow him his say.

"What *exactly* will doom me?" I asked.

"You're curious too."

"Nope. I'm afraid I'm not."

"Really?" My prisoner gave a sneaky smile. *"Why did you become a Goner? Question what things? Just what will doom me?"*

"That's not curiosity," I protested. "That's making conversation."

"With a *Goner*?"

Damn. He had me again.

"I might be inquisitive but I'm not stupid!" I blurted. "What did you hope to achieve? There's no place to live but this island. Nowhere for you to run *to*."

"You sure about that?"

"The Town Council have sent a dozen exploration groups west, all the way to America. Nothing has changed. Nobody can survive there."

"What about the east? None of the scouting teams returned from the east."

"Yeah. Which means it must be even *more* dangerous." I countered. "Or do you think they found a wild party and couldn't be bothered coming back?"

This guy was an idiot. Over a hundred years without a radio broadcast, a plane, a boat or even a message in a bottle from east *or* west.

New Hebrides was well and truly on its own.

We sat silently for a while. I could tell the Goner was cooking up another argument and, I had to admit, I was intrigued as to what nonsense he'd spout next.

"Why do the authorities try to stop us getting away at all?" he asked finally. "If all we're heading for is oblivion?"

"The population can't be allowed to fluctuate." *Everyone* knew that. "We have limited resources and energy, so we need an exact number of people for the island to be able to function at maximum efficiency. That's why deserting carries an automatic death penalty."

The boy bit his lip. He probably didn't need reminding of that fact.

"Yet we still run," he pointed out. "So why is the shoreline the least patrolled part of the island?"

"Eh? Because the really important stuff is in the middle." I couldn't see where he was going with this.

"Which doesn't need to be guarded, does it? It's surrounded by army barracks."

This was true.

"We Regulators patrol the perimeter." I was determined to give as good as I got. "And there are armed Navals on any coracles that go fishing."

"Coracles which aren't locked when they're not being used." The boy stuck out his jaw. "Think about it! If there was absolutely no chance of me getting off the island, I wouldn't have tried. Nobody in their right mind would."

While I was pondering this, the Goner kicked me in the stomach.

I doubled over, spluttering, and he jumped and spun in mid-air. His foot caught me square in the jaw and I flew backwards, colliding with a stack of barrels. As the boy raced towards me, I instinctively drew my baton and he veered off and headed for the village instead. But it's hard to flee with hands fastened behind your back. I caught up with him on the outskirts, wrested my adversary to the deck and sat on him.

"Gotta admire your perseverance." I massaged my stinging jaw. "You would have made a good Regulator."

"I *am* a Regulator, you fool!"

I shook my head in bewilderment. The kid could fight, no doubt about it. But why would a *Regulator* become a Goner?

My prisoner started in with the questions again. I was too busy trying to get my breath back to object.

"As you say, deserters are automatically executed," he grunted. "So, if the Council aren't squeamish about killing us, why aren't you issued with guns rather than stunners? It would have saved a lot of time and effort if you'd been able to just shoot me."

To be honest, that *had* occurred to me more than once.

"I don't know," I admitted.

"And why use a bunch of kids to hunt Goners down rather than armed Lawmen?

"Hey! I have a good success rate," I replied defensively. "I caught you."

"Just. And you almost died in the attempt."

My head was beginning to hurt. And not simply from the kick.

"It's almost as if the government *wants* to give us a fighting chance." The Goner persisted. "If someone has the guts to try and get off the island, they genuinely have a chance of succeeding. Why would our leaders *allow* that?"

Another good point. I was totally regretting getting into this argument.

"The Town Council are lying about what's out there." The Goner made one last attempt to convince me. "They've altered the historical records to cover up their deceit."

"Why bother? Nobody looks at them anyhow." I motioned the boy to his feet, keeping my distance this time. "Most of the population can't even *read*."

"I can. *I've* seen the records. And I know some of them are fake." He nodded at the sea. "The clue is in the *fish*."

"Well, that's nice and vague."

"I could be specific. But you won't believe me unless you find out the truth for yourself."

A gust of wind blew across the dock and I shivered. The boy's top was lying a few feet away and I realised he must be freezing.

"Let's get you out of here before you catch your death of cold." I winced. "Sorry. Bad choice of phrase."

I took off my jacket and draped it over his shoulders.

"What's your name, anyway?" I asked.

"Why should you care?"

"I'm curious," I shrugged. "Like you keep pointing out."

"Elvis Regulator Presley," he responded, using his formal title.

"John Regulator Wayne." I held out my hand, forgetting for a second that my quarry was handcuffed. "Sorry how things turned out."

"Not as damned sorry as me. And I know exactly what you're called."

That took me by surprise. So did his next statement.

"I would have let you fall back there. But you're too important."

"Oh, stop." I put a hand to my cheek. "You're giving me a big head."

"When you discover your real identity, you'll desert as well." The boy smiled grimly. "Unless the Town Council find out who you are first. Then they'll kill you."

All right. This conversation had gone way past nonsense and moved firmly into treason.

"Don't say another word," I snapped. "Or I'll switch this baton on and shove it up your nose."

I took my captor by the arm and silently marched him to Justice Hall. Then I went home.

As was normal, the Goner would be tried and executed the next day.

I have to admit, it's difficult to get facts about the past. Everyone knows the world was destroyed by the Golden Plague and we only survived by isolating ourselves on the island of New Hebrides. But we've been here a long time, so the rest of earth's history is a bit fuzzy.

Part of the reason is that there are no books on the island – they take up too much valuable space. The Town Council has digital records, of course, but they're kind of irrelevant now that the world has gone. New Hebrideans work too hard to waste time poring over what once was and, like I said, most of us don't bother learning to read unless our job requires it. Regulators and Lawmen can, of course, because we have to fill out reports. But it's boring and I can't imagine that anyone ever looked at books for fun, no matter what the old folks say.

Dad and Mum insist it's dumb to dwell on the past because it was such a horrible place, though we pass down stories by word of mouth to amuse ourselves. My favourite is about some guy called Norah who put a bunch of creatures on a big boat to save them and sailed it round the world. But there are no animals on New Hebrides, so it couldn't have landed here. Maybe it sank and that's why there's only marine life left.

The clue is in the fish. That's what the Goner had said. Only I didn't know what on earth he meant.

My father is a Lawman, Inspector Grade, so he has a lot of exciting tales about his job. Much better than history, I bet. Last week, for instance, he caught a man smuggling whale bile across the island in his underwear.

Lawmen are what we Regulators become when we're old enough to pass the entrance exam. If we fail, however, we end up as Green Fingers in the Towers. The Towers are almost a thousand feet high and that's where everything is grown. Apples. Wheat. Soya. Potatoes. There are even trees on the top. Green Fingers water, weed and harvest the crops and aren't allowed to leave the place.

Being a Green Finger's not a bad life, I guess, but it's shameful. The Towers stink of seaweed fertilizer and failure. Plus, there's the guilt factor. Because the population is strictly controlled, the oldest Green Finger is removed to make way for any Regulator or Military Cadet who fails the exam. Nobody knows where the wrinklies go, but the word *recycling* gets bandied about. Naturally, new apprentices in the Towers aren't very popular and spend the first few years spreading muck with their bare hands.

That's not the worst part. The worst part is that the Lawman or Soldier gets a replacement son. One that, hopefully, *can* follow in his footsteps.

"Evening, boy." My father looked up as I entered. "Hunt down anyone interesting today?"

You can see where I get my sense of humour from.

"Would you like some Teaweed?" Mother turned from the stove. "It's just brewed."

"No thanks, Mum."

"How's the revision going?" Dad asked casually.

It was a loaded question. Robert Lawman Burns is well respected. In his eyes, I cannot be allowed to fail. It would reflect badly on him.

Well, two can play at that game.

"Have you ever seen the Town Council's historical records?" I said, equally nonchalant.

My mother put a hand over her mouth.

"Why would I want to?" Dad bristled. "What relevance would it have to my job?"

"The Goner I caught today said some were faked. Insisted he had proof."

"What exactly *was* that proof?" Father's mouth tightened.

"Beats me," I lied. "I wasn't daft enough to ask."

Mum looked relieved. She blew a wisp of greying hair from her forehead and got some mugs from the larder.

Quite often, what my mind thinks and what my mouth says are two entirely separate things. This was one of those occasions. I was tired and sore and dispirited or I'd never have pushed it.

"What if *we* asked to see them?" I ploughed on. "Maybe we could find a clue as to why Goners think the way they do. Wouldn't it be easier to stop them beforehand than to hunt them once they make their move?"

Father was on his feet and round the table with a speed that belied his size. His hand swung in an arc towards my head.

I blocked it with my forearm.

Dad lashed out with his foot and my chair rattled away, tipping me onto the floor. I rolled under the table and bounced up on the other side.

No time to think. Slamming my hands on the tablecloth, I arched my back and somersaulted, bringing both heels down on Dad's shoulders. My father sank to his knees with a grunt. I completed the manoeuvre, springing back onto the table and adopting a fighting stance.

"Watch my tablecloth!" Mum admonished, trying to rescue the plates. "It's the only one we have."

Oh. She just *had* to say that.

With a sneaky grin, Dad yanked the woven covering towards him. I was catapulted backwards in a hail of spinning plastic bowls and cutlery, landing heavily on my back. My father got one burly shoulder under the table and stood upright with a triumphant roar. I slid off and landed on the floor as Dad surged forwards, ramming the up-turned table against the wall, trapping me behind it. By the time I had struggled free, he was in the middle of the kitchen, a fish knife in his calloused fist.

Mum stood with her back to the stove, watching apprehensively.

I pulled the baton from my belt and advanced. Father raised his eyebrows, twirling the knife expertly. But I'd had a bad day and I wasn't going to back down.

Sparks flew as the knife and baton connected over and over. Flash, crackle, bang. We whirled and ducked and parried across the kitchen floor.

My father is an experienced fighter, but I was young and mad about the cowardice I'd shown that day. I reckoned I could take him.

I might have thought that through a bit more.

Slowly, I was forced to retreat until I was against the wall again. Dad's arms were a blur, his eyes manic.

Then Mum hit him across the head with her kettle.

"Marie!" He sank to his knees again, clutching his scalp. I stepped forward and raised the stunner with a victorious yell. Mum tipped the kettle and hot water cascaded down my leg.

"Oooooow!" I hopped around, clutching my thigh. "I said I didn't want tea!"

"Shut up." My mother slapped the weapon from my hand. "Don't you dare try that kind of dirty move on your father."

"You just clonked him with a teapot!"

"He's my husband. He's used to it."

She pulled Dad to his feet.

"As for you, Robert Inspector Burns?" She deliberately included his middle title, which meant she was really annoyed. "I've told you a million times not to fight at mealtimes. The fishcakes are ruined."

"Really? I can never tell." Dad rolled his eyes at me and Mum raised the kettle again. "Just joking, darling!"

"You pair get out of my sight while I clean this place up." Mother surveyed the wrecked kitchen with a heartfelt groan. "You both need to cool off."

"Boy has to learn to expect the unexpected." My father put his arm round my shoulders and steered me to the door. "But I'm quietly confident, he'll pass the exam."

He winked at me.

"The combat part, anyway."

"Damned right." I bent to retrieve my stunner. Glanced up.

I was just in time to catch the exchange that passed fleetingly between my parents. It only lasted a second, but I recognised it instantly. I'd seen it in the eyes of fleeing Goners when they glanced back at me.

It was a look of naked fear.

-4-

We live in New Hebrides' Fourth Ring, which is mostly residential, the only area where the population has a proper mixture of occupations. The centre of the island holds the Town Council buildings and Technological Hub and you need a pass to go there. Ring One is administrative and military, mostly serving and guarding the centre. Ring Two is the Green Zone, where the Towers loom over everything like jagged concrete teeth. Ring Three contains the retail sector and light industry. Then there's us, Ring Four, a mixed bag, like I said. Ring Five is on the perimeter, the largest area and entirely given over to heavy industry and fishing. Understandable, since we live on an island.

And of course, there's the legendary Sixth Ring, a narrow tubular band which encircles New Hebrides. According to legend, it was once above the water but rising sea levels eventually submerged it. Many people don't believe it actually exists, but fishermen sometimes claim to see its shadowy form under the waves. Whatever the truth, nobody but the Town Council knows what it is or what it ever did.

I wondered if *that* was in their records?

At Dad's suggestion, we cycled to the Second Ring and eventually ended up in a concrete square called Hitchcock Park. We didn't talk on the journey, but that was fine, for I was too confused to speak.

I'd never seen my father afraid before.

Dad led me to a bench and pulled a clockwork lantern from his bag. The place was deserted. It was getting dark and New Hebrides has a curfew. Most of the power goes off after 8.00pm to conserve energy and the only people allowed out in the evening are Regulators, Lawmen, Military and night fishermen.

"What happened today?" he said finally.

"Told you. I caught a Goner."

"Well done. What's that, three now?" My father nudged my arm. "You're going to make Inspector someday."

"He was called Elvis Regulator Presley." I emphasised the middle title.

"Don't know the name," Dad replied evenly. "His father's not from my precinct, thank goodness. That would make lunch in the canteen fairly awkward."

"I never heard of a Regulator deserting."

"It's not something The Town Council likes to advertise," Dad shrugged. "But Regulators are

Lawmen in training. And Lawmen are suspicious by nature. Our job is to ask questions."

He looked up at the moonlight shimmering across the solar panels that topped most of the buildings. "Often we're not too fond of what we find."

I didn't like the way he said that.

"Why did you bring me way out here to talk?" I asked. Then a sinister thought occurred to me. "Is our house *bugged*?"

I suppose I'm suspicious by nature too.

"Probably not." Dad stroked his beard. "The Council doesn't have the means to monitor the population anymore, which is why Goners are on the increase. But Lawmen are powerful and we're armed, so it's possible."

He leaned in close to me.

"That's why you mustn't talk about wanting to see the historical records. Not indoors, anyway. You almost gave your mother a heart attack."

So *that's* what I'd done wrong.

"We're *allowed* to look at them." I couldn't understand what all the fuss was about. "Sure, we have to fill in a million forms and sign a confidentiality agreement, but it's not illegal."

"What if the Goner was right?" Dad said. "What if some *are* faked?"

I caught my breath. I had to be very careful here.

"What you've just said is very close to treason." I stammered. "I have to report *any* criticism of the Town Council to the authorities. Even from you. *Especially* from you."

"Good boy." Father didn't seem too concerned. "Don't worry, I'm just testing. Part of your exam revision. Now, think through what I've just told you."

Thank God for that.

"All right. Why bother to fake records?" I tapped my lip slowly. "Why not just deny access to them?"

"Because people who become Goners have a certain way of thinking," Dad grinned. "They're selfish. It's not good enough for them that everyone has security and employment. They want change for the sake of change and can't accept that, under the circumstances, this is the best society we can manage. That New Hebrides has to stay exactly as it is."

I have to admit, I've never been very close to my father. He has his job and I have mine. I couldn't recall a time when we had just sat in the park, wrapped in night, talking to each other. It was quite nice.

So I opened my mouth before I thought. Again.

"How do we know this is the best society we can manage?" I asked. "If nothing ever changes?"

My father's head shot round, eyes sparkling in the darkness.

"Yes," he hissed. "That's exactly the way a Goner thinks. And I should report *you* for saying something so subversive."

Suddenly I was aware what a deadly game we were playing.

"I didn't mean it like that," I spluttered, trying to recover the advantage. "I'm trying to think the way my enemy thinks."

"Commendable. But you don't have to say what the enemy says." He tapped my chin. "That's a reportable offence, though I'll let you off this time."

Suddenly I didn't feel close to my father anymore.

"Back to the test." Dad swept his arm around the park. "Pop quiz. Suppose there's a Prowler in this park, robbing people late at night. How do you catch him?"

I knew I had to redeem myself and thought hard.

"I'm guessing the surveillance cameras don't have power anymore, so I'd have Lawmen hidden round the perimeter. Next time the Prowler robs someone, they move in together and surround him."

"Not an effective use of manpower." Dad stretched out his legs and put his hands behind his head. "We can't have valuable people sitting around, night after night, waiting for one measly Prowler. There's not enough of us."

All right. That made sense. I racked my brains for another solution.

"You make him come to you," I said finally. "Put one Lawman in the park, disguised as a help-less Citizen. Carrying goods or something. An easy target."

"Outstanding." Dad patted me on the arm. "You set a trap."

Then it hit me.

"The *records* are a trap," I breathed. "Only truly doubtful people will ask to see them. Potential Goners."

"Like I say, you'll make Inspector someday," Dad nodded. Then his face became serious.

"If you make an official request to see the records, you'll be flagged up as a possible dissident and end up shuffling manure in the Towers. Do you understand?"

"I do." I really did.

Dad patted me on the cheek.

"I don't want a new son. I like the one I have just fine."

I considered myself warned.

Yet, on the way home, my mind was churning.

I liked my life. Wanted to follow in my father's footsteps and become a respected Investigator.

But what good was that, if there was a limit to what I could investigate?

-5-

Regulators don't just hunt down Goners. We keep an eye on everything. Report suspicious behaviour and anti-Government talkers. Ration cheats. Slackers. Illegal fishing. Smugglers. Curfew breakers.

That's why we don't have any friends.

I'm one of the best. I can sniff out a lie or smell fear on someone's skin. I'm a bit of a Bulldog in many ways. Once I get my teeth into something, I can't let it go.

There are no animals on New Hebrides, like I said, except rats. But Bulldogs, apparently, were pets that humans once kept in their houses. A bulldog would love them and protect them and… once it got its teeth into something never let it go, I suppose.

I know what a Bulldog looks like because our neighbour, Alexander Bootmaker Bell, has an ancient painting on his wall of one playing Poker with some other dogs. I think it must be some kind of joke, but I don't get it and neither does he.

Alexander Bootmaker Bell is very old. Maybe a hundred. But he's allowed to live because he can still make boots. That's the way it works in New Hebrides. You're all right as long as you're useful. But if you get too old or too sick to work you're put to sleep, just like dogs used to be. Then your body is used as fertilizer in the Towers or made into bait for catching Humble-Squid. On the upside, some family then gets to have another child, because we have to keep the population stable.

It sounds harsh, but it can't be any other way. Nothing can be wasted.

We have enough drains on our, already stretched, recourses. Every six months the whole island is irradiated, in case spores from the Golden Plague have drifted across the sea and reached New Hebrides. It takes up a huge amount of power but it has kept the menace at bay for over a century.

Unfortunately, it also makes the population sterile.

Nobody here can have kids the way they used to. Instead, new Citizens are grown from DNA banks stored in the Technological Centre. Only the plants in the Towers, high above the island and carefully sealed inside glass casings to protect them from irradiation, can reproduce naturally.

Thank God for that, or we'd be eating nothing but sea creatures our whole lives.

The clue is in the fish.

What the hell did Elvis Regulator Presley mean by that? I couldn't get it out of my head. The Goner was right, damn him. I *was* curious.

I'd been well and truly put off asking to see the historical records. So where would I get new information without looking like a troublemaker?

I thought about Alexander Bootmaker Bell and his picture. What about a really old person? They might remember stories the rest of us didn't. Then again, what would stop one informing on me if I started asking awkward questions?

Suddenly the alarm sirens went off, shattering my thoughts.

Oh my God. The thing every New Hebridean dreads.

A hurricane coming in from the east. And during Humble-Squid season!

I ran for the shoreline, though every fibre of my being wanted to head in the other direction - up to higher ground, near the centre of the island, where I'd be safe. After all, the Fishermen know how to handle bad weather and I don't.

It's not that I'm afraid of water. I reckon I'm one of the best swimmers on the island. There are no real predators off the west coast, for reasons I've never understood, so I swim there most days as a way of building up my muscles.

But a hurricane was coming from the east and it generates giant waves.

Waves filled, at this time of year, with Humble-Squid.

I had no way of knowing when the storm would hit, but it had to be close. At one time, New Hebrides used tracker buoys to warn of incoming danger but we no longer had the juice to keep them on.

The wind was picking up as I reached the Fifth Ring. Desperate men, women and children were battening everything down and securing the Coracles with ropes, their faces grey and tense. They wanted to flee as well, but fishing was their livelihood. If their houses and boats were destroyed, they'd starve - and so would a lot more of us.

I was in a better position than most of the people round me. The island was ringed with fishing rigs, some of them forty feet high - used for bulk net catches and landing Monster Fish. I had been designated defender on rig number 4B.

The rain was already lashing my face as I reached my destination and began to climb the ladder. My heart was hammering, not least because I'd almost fallen to my death from an identical structure. I felt a pang of guilt, remembering how Elvis Presley had rescued me. Or maybe it was just the icy water.

On top of the structure stood a mounted pulse gun. I pulled a key from a chain around my neck, unlocked the mechanism and pointed the barrel into the air. Squeezed the trigger and watched a bright blue burst of energy shoot into the sky.

It was working, though pulse guns normally have no energy. I believe I've mentioned our lack of resources several times. But this was a serious emergency and all available power had been diverted to where it was needed.

A gust of wind almost whisked me from my perch and I grabbed the crossbar with a yelp of fear.

Deja Vous.

This was going to be a big one. I climbed onto the cab seat, strapped myself in, readied the gun and put my eye to the sight. The lens was treated with some kind of coating that repelled water, so I had a chance of seeing what I was aiming at. Pity the powers that be couldn't have provided me with clothing made of the same stuff. I was soaked to the skin already.

Then I saw the first wave and it was huge.

The people below spotted it too. They gave up fastening down things and clung to the nearest solid structure they could find, some of them worming their way under the ropes. All looked up at me fearfully. I was the only person who could save them now.

The wave washed over the jetties like a foaming blanket and I began to fire into the torrent of water.

Squid. Fire. Squid. Fire. Squid. Fire. Thank God the sights narrowed my field of vision, so I couldn't see the extent of the carnage. Even so...

I watched one man engulfed whole by a ten foot specimen, so I blew it to pieces. Another running with smaller squid swallowing his arms. I missed him as he slipped and plunged, screaming, between the piers and into the ocean.

The rain was stinging my own arms now, hard enough to bring up weals on the skin. But I couldn't think about that.

Sight. Fire. Sight. Fire. Sight. Fire.

Two fire engines arrived. The Firemen leapt out, uncoiled their hoses and began blasting the creatures over the side. I laid down covering fire until I was sure they could handle themselves. Swung the scope in an arc, facing out to sea.

My head jerked back. Another wave coming in, much larger this time. The firemen climbed back into their vehicle and retreated.

Then it hit and I was shooting again. The barrel of my gun sizzled in the torrential rain, sending up clouds of steam. One man staggered out of a fishing hut with a squid enveloping his head like a comical hat. I blasted the poor guy off his feet. Eaten alive was no way to die.

And then the third wave. I knew this had to be the last one. I knew because it was a wall of water bigger than I could have imagined.

"Come on!" I screamed. "Do your worst! I am a BULLDOG!"

I raked the wave over and over until it crashed into the village. For a few seconds, the whole community was submerged. The wave receded, revealing the full horror of what it left behind.

Fishermen were fighting dozens of Humble-Squid with everything they could lay their hands on. Marlinspikes. Fishing nets. Bare hands.

I gritted my teeth. No matter how often I fired there was another monstrosity to aim at, each one crushing a man or woman with its tentacles or biting off limbs. There would be a lot of new inhabitants being incubated soon.

I caught a flash of grey, impossibly large in my viewfinder. The scope couldn't take it all in. I leaned to the side, wiping rain from my eyes.

A giant, armoured squid, almost fifteen feet long, was stranded on top of one of the processing sheds. On the roof opposite crouched a little girl.

"Oh, no…."

I fired again and again but the squid's casing was too thick pierce. The creature was slowly choking to death in the air, too preoccupied with its own predicament to see the potential quarry. But these things don't die easily. It would spot her before it expired and swallow the girl whole, just to be mean.

"Up on the roof!" I yelled at the throng below. "There's a kid on the roof!"

My words were whisked away by the howling wind.

I raised my hands to the heavens, cursing the leaden sky.

Above me was a narrow wire strut, sloping from the top of the rig, right over the roof of the shed to the pier beyond.

I thought of Elvis Regulator Presley.

Well. Anything *he* could do, I could do better.

Aiming as carefully as I could I fired a bolt at the little girl. It blasted a hole in the corrugated iron, right next to her. She leapt back, looked up and spotted me, biting one knuckle and shuffling from side to side.

Unstrapping myself, I pulled off my top and wrapped it round the cable. Then, before I could lose my nerve, I launched myself into the air.

I rocketed down the wire. The squid spotted me and raised its tentacles as I passed overhead. They snapped together with a force strong enough to crush the life from me, but I had already let go of the jacket.

I landed next to the girl with a cry of pain and scooped her into my arms.

"Hold on to me. Tight!"

The kid wrapped her legs round my waist and I dropped into the hole as the tentacles descended, splintering the roof into jagged shards.

I plummeted down, landing on my back in a pile of soggy fishing nets. A whoosh of air escaped my lungs and I saw stars.

Oh Jeez! That *hurt*.

"Want to get off me now?" I wheezed. "You just crushed a part of my anatomy that cannot be named in young company."

The girl hugged me tighter.

Eventually, I gave up struggling and squeezed her back.

My father was still helping with the mopping up when I limped home. Mum took one look at me and insisted I go straight to bed.

I woke next morning, stiff and sore, to find Dad sitting on the edge of my bunk.

"You're a bit of a hero in the Hemmingway fishing village," he said. "Risking your life to save a little girl."

"Really?" I had to admit I felt pretty good about that. It wasn't often that Regulators got a compliment.

Then I saw my father's expression and the grin faded from my face.

"Get up." He threw a fresh set of clothes at me.

"You're in a whole heap of trouble."

<h1 style="text-align:center">-6-</h1>

We ended up back in Hitchcock Park, on the same bench. Mum had given us a packed lunch and waved uneasily from the doorway as we left.

Dad handed me a honey-topped cake, a rare luxury. Perhaps this lecture wasn't going to be as bad as I thought.

My father looked round cautiously before speaking.

"The Goner you caught yesterday?" He bit into a slab of dried kelp. "At his trial, he insisted you gave him a head start."

Oh. This lecture was going to be *worse* than I thought.

"I would never do that," I lied. "I'm not lying, I swear."

"And nobody would take the word of a Goner over a Regulator," Dad replied grimly. "If there hadn't been a witness."

"What?" My heart plunged into an ocean of dread. Who could possibly have seen us?

"A Council maintenance worker was inspecting one of the gun cabs, you ass." My father breathed deeply, trying to keep his temper under control. "He saw the whole thing. Watched you engage the Goner in conversation too."

"It was one mistake," I pleaded. "Well, two mistakes. But the kid had just saved my life!"

"He reported that too. And you caught the boy and turned him over in the end, so your indiscretions might have been overlooked." Dad chewed the seaweed furiously. "Except the very next day you abandon your gun post!"

"I was rescuing a helpless little girl!" But I knew that wasn't going to wash.

"You were showing off!" Dad roared. "You could have saved a dozen more people by staying where you were! The majority over the individual - it's a prime rule, John!" He slapped me across the head. "What were you thinking?"

"What's going to happen to me?" I asked quietly, handing him back the uneaten treat.

"There *was* talk of arresting you." Dad put it carefully in his satchel, for nothing is wasted on the island. "I pulled strings and stopped that happening. You'll even remain a Regulator until the exam in two weeks."

I felt relief wash over me.

"But I very much doubt the authorities will give you a pass mark."

Oh no.

"I'm going to the Towers?"

"It seems likely." Dad took a sip of water from a glass bottle and folded up his own lunch. I saw that his hands were shaking. "I'm only 40, so I'll be given another child from the DNA base. A new son."

"Can't you do something? *Please.*"

"I cannot," he said regretfully. "I tried my best, of course. But I don't have enough influence to sway an exam board."

I understood and appreciated that he had even attempted it. You don't make waves in New Hebrides, no matter how esteemed you are.

"I'd like to be on my own for a while, Dad," I said. "Do you mind?"

"Of course not. I have to go home and tell your mother." He stood up clenching and unclenching his fists. "Not that she hasn't guessed. That's why you got the fancy cake."

He leaned over and kissed me quickly on the head. I looked up, surprised.

"Just remember you are my son," he whispered. "You will always be my son."

He strode away without looking back.

At first I just cried, salty tears sliding over my cheeks and spasms shaking my body. I got up and paced up and down. I'd risked my life to help that girl! And I was being *punished* for it?

Then I reproached myself. You break the rules, you pay the price. As a Regulator I knew that better than anyone. Two days ago I had been the rising star of my division. Now, quite rightly, I looked like a maverick who couldn't be trusted in a crisis.

Hell. I'd ruined my own life and that was that. No point in complaining or getting mad about it.

"This is so unfair!" I screamed, kicking the bench until a slab of rusting paint fell off. "It's not right! Well… maybe it is. But not when it happens to me!"

I finally ran out of energy and sat back down, head in hands. Then I cried some more.

Once I'd used up every useless emotion, I began to think.

Could I possibly figure a way out of this mess?

I had two weeks left as a Regulator before I was destined to spend the rest of my life knee deep in crap. What if I did something spectacular in that time? Something that would put me back in the Council's good graces?

I remembered the other thing Elvis Regulator Presley had whispered to me.

The Town Council are lying about what's out there. I found proof!

Perhaps I could go to my superiors and tell them that part of our conversation. They could interrogate the boy and…

I quickly dismissed the idea. All it proved was that I'd listened to a Goner criticizing the Town Council, which wouldn't exactly help my position. Besides, the boy must be dead by now.

Then it hit me.

Elvis Presley looked younger than me. Must have just started as a Regulator. He didn't even have the nerve or the sense to let me die and save his own skin.

But *he* found proof that the Council was lying?

Not without help, he didn't. Someone pointed him in the right direction. He was part of a group, I was sure of it.

Suppose I tracked down that gang and handed them over? It would prove my loyalty and dedication to the job. And it would remove potential fuel for future Goners.

It was a risky strategy but better than growing potatoes for a living.

I might have thought that through a bit more.

It was getting dark when I arrived home. Mum and Dad were sitting at the kitchen table, waiting. Mother's eyes were red-rimmed and, as I came through the door, she leapt up and hugged me tight.

"Oh my boy!" she wailed, her face pressed against my chest. "The Towers won't be so bad, I promise."

I didn't see how she could promise something like that, never having been near one. The weeping wasn't encouraging either.

I prized her away.

"I'd like that cake now," I said. "I'm feeling a bit peckish."

"Your father ate it." She shot Dad a filthy look.

"Didn't think you'd get your appetite back so soon." My father stroked his beard thoughtfully. "Mind you, if you're going to be munching nothing but fruit for the rest of your life…."

"Robert Burns!" Mum picked up the kettle. "How *dare* you?"

"Relax, Marie." Dad squinted at me. "I think our boy has a plan."

Yup. My father is an excellent Inspector.

"I do indeed," I agreed. "I've no intention of going to the Towers."

"You're not thinking of *deserting*!" Mum's face turned white and she swung the kettle towards me. She was better with that thing than I was with my baton.

"Of course not!" I raised my hands in surrender. "I reckon I have a way to get back into the Council's favour, is all."

"A big bust, I imagine." My father nodded approvingly. "What's your lead? How can I help?"

"You can't." I saw my mother's face fall, but I steeled myself. "I have to do this entirely on my own or I won't have proved my worth."

"For goodness sakes, talk to him, Robert!" Mum waved the kettle back and forth between us. "Make the lad see sense."

"He's right," Dad replied quietly. "If the authorities suspect my hand in whatever he's doing, he won't get the credit. John has to succeed on his own."

"Oh. Why don't I make you another cake then?" Mum began opening cupboards, so I wouldn't see her tears. "I'm sure I have enough ingredients left."

"Come outside boy." Dad beckoned to me.

We sat on the stoop next to each other. It was growing cold.

"Are you being brave or do you really have a scheme?" Dad patted me on the knee. "Be honest."

"I have a plan. I have a good plan." I glanced hopefully at him. "And you *could* help from behind the scenes if you wanted."

"I only offered to make your mother feel better." Dad rubbed his forehead awkwardly. "I have the feeling what you're about to undertake is… risky. I'm afraid I've caused enough trouble on your behalf already. If I got caught helping, I'd be demoted. Or worse. Then what would happen to Mum?"

He was right, of course. Though it still hurt.

"But you do whatever it takes. Break heads. Be ruthless." Dad hesitated.

"Kill if you have to."

He looked sideways at me.

"You've got nothing to lose."

His warning couldn't be plainer.

Then he went back indoors and left me in the dark.

-7-

I'm no expert on history. Got little use for it, as I said.

The Town Council do their best to keep the past alive, I suppose. At birth, they give us names of people who were once famous, but it means nothing to most Citizens. I've no idea who John Wayne was in the old world and neither does Dad. Mum thinks he might have been a cowboy or a boxer, though why someone who makes boxes should be well known is beyond me.

But there is one person the Citizens will always remember.

Alan Carver.

He's the reason New Hebrides exists.

Once there was a whole world full of people, not just our island. It wasn't a nice world, as far as I can tell. War. Famine. Poverty. Pollution. And it got worse as humans began to use up all the natural resources the planet had to offer.

Alan Carver tried to make it better.

Nobody knows much about his personal life, for Carver was an intensely private man. Despite that, he built up an enormous business empire then, suddenly, began to plough all his money into a field called renewable energy. Smart move. With the word's oil and gas running out, it made him a billionaire.

He bought a small island in the Atlantic Ocean and filled it with state-of-the-art labs and top scientists. The 'Carver Foundation' began to work on ever more ambitious projects, trying to usher in a Golden Age for mankind.

What we got was the Golden Plague.

At the time, there were laboratories all over the world, working on genetically modified food. I'm no scientist but I guess the concept was simple enough. If you could make quick-growing, fast reproducing, hardy crops that required little water or nutrition, you could solve global food shortages. Though Alan Carver was tireless in his warnings about unregulated experiments, other countries went ahead with their own research.

Nobody knows how the first spores escaped. But, within months, genetically modified wheat began to spring up in a place called Australia. It overwhelmed all the other crops. Then it appeared on the beaches. In the desert. Finally, it took over the cities, forcing its way through cracks in the pavements and walls.

The wheat was unkillable. Pesticides didn't affect it and, if you burned the stalks down, they sprang back even stronger. It was self-pollinating, which means the crop reproduced itself without the help of insects, I think. I'm not even sure what an insect is. And the wheat quickly developed a defence mechanism that nobody could have predicted.

It became inedible.

Before long, this Supergrass had wiped out all the other crops in Australia, turning the country into a sea of waving sheaves. Animals starved first. Then people.

Worse was to come. The vast fields released enormous pollen clouds that smothered everything alive. Flash fires wiped out entire states. The continent of Australia was eventually quarantined but, by then, it was too late.

The Golden Plague started cropping up in neighbouring countries, its spores drifting across the ocean on the wind. Governments sealed their borders, but the wheat continued to advance. International bodies united to find a way to kill it.

Nothing worked.

Alan Carver saw the whole planet was in danger of being overrun - but his own island was isolated and virtually self-sufficient. So he used the rest of his vast fortune to fortify the hastily named New Hebrides. He hired a private army and bought aircraft and weapons. He flew out craftsmen, mechanics and anyone else he thought would be useful until the island was full.

The Carver Foundation invented an Irradiation Machine, the only thing that *did* kill the wheat. But it wasn't strong enough to cover more than the few square miles of New Hebrides.

And it made the inhabitants sterile.

Carver, again, had a solution. That guy thought of *everything*.

His teams collected DNA samples of remaining humans and animals and stored them on the island in huge banks. They were to be used for creating future generations that could repopulate the world.

If the Golden Plague could be destroyed.

Yet he never made it to New Hebrides himself. Carver remained in a fortified compound in a place called Atlantic City, working desperately on a solution for the Golden Plague. One that remained stubbornly beyond his grasp. All around him the eastern seaboard of what was called America descended into the Great Chaos, as the remnants of humanity fought each other to escape in any boat or aircraft they could find.

He waited too long. The helicopter sent to get him was loading the last DNA samples when the Foundation's compound was breached. Carver was overtaken and killed by a rampaging mob before he could reach the chopper.

The last days were pretty rough for the Citizens of the island. They couldn't allow thousands of floating refugees to swamp New Hebrides, so they blew any incoming craft out of the sea. Kept doing it until nobody else came.

Now we're all that's left of the human race.

The irradiation machine helps stop the Golden Plague gaining a foothold in New Hebrides but uses power we can ill afford. It takes all our meagre raw materials and ingenuity to maintain the technology we have. For well over a hundred years, the Town Council's scientists have tried to find a way to kill the wheat so we can reclaim the world. But it's an uphill battle. It looks like we're stuck here.

Put that in your pipe and smoke it, Elvis Regulator Presley.

And yet... I couldn't stop thinking about what he had said.

The Town Council are lying about what's out there.

The clue is in the fish.

-8-

Regulators tend to be solitary types. Or we hang out with each other since nobody wants to be our buddies. Most people don't talk to us at all, in case they say something wrong, which we are duty bound to report.

Still, I have one ally. I met her a month ago and we got on pretty well. Her name is Florence Mower Nightingale and she's obviously in the wrong job.

Any idiot can mow. It's just walking round and round the island and crawling into nooks and crannies, looking for signs that wheat spores have taken hold. If they find a couple of stalks, they pull them up and report the infestation. Then the area is wiped with a handheld Irradiation Machine.

It's the lowest rung on the ladder, yet Florence is smart as hell. Tramping round the island bent double is a complete waste of her talents.

Can't be helped, I suppose. At first, the DNA samples Alan Carver collected for New Hebrides were carefully labelled. That way, scientists on the island could be given children whose DNA came from scientists of the past. Soldiers got kids from the genetic banks of people who had once been in the military. You get the picture.

But in the last days of the evacuations to New Hebrides, Carver's men scrambled to get samples from anyone they could find, with no time to categorise them. My guess is Florence is one of those 'Unidentifieds'.

So, when she complains about her lot, I let it slide. It's a minor infraction and she's the only pal I've got. I also let her off when she sasses me. Which is often.

I met her for lunch in the Retail Ring. I bought some Calamari from a stall and we sat on the concrete pavement with our backs against a Potter's store.

"I need your help," I said. "Or else I'm headed for the Towers."

"Ooh. Can you get me some tomatoes?" Florence swept a lock of jet-black hair from her grubby forehead. "They taste salty, but they're full of nutrition."

"Sure." I sulked. "I'll throw a couple off the 50th floor balcony for you to catch. Tied to a large rock."

"You're not kidding then."

"I'm not."

"Sorry, John." She wolfed down another handful of calamari. Mowers only get minimal rations and she's always hungry. "What do you want me to do?"

"You travel all over this island. I'd like you to start asking about a Regulator called Elvis Presley. Who he met with. Where he went."

"Wouldn't you be best qualified to do that?"

"He became a Goner," I explained. "I'll hit a dead end at every turn. Nobody will admit knowing him."

"You want to tell me the whole story?"

So I did. Including my plan.

"You almost died twice in the last two days." Florence looked sideways at me. "This is risky too. Would working in the Towers be so bad?"

"Do you like Mowing?" I retorted. "When you're easily smart enough to be a Scientist?"

"I get to work with my hands," she said sarcastically. "Lots of fresh air."

"Which is about all you have to eat."

"I won't help because you *feed* me!" she grunted. "I'll do it cause I owe you."

This was true. I'd first encountered her being beaten in an alleyway by a couple of Prowlers because she refused to hand over her meagre rations. I fought them off and carried her home. Seeing her bruises, I figured she'd learned her lesson so I did a deal with her. I wouldn't report her breaking the curfew if she'd snoop around for me whenever I asked. Thought it would help with my advancement to Inspector.

I guess I really do like to break rules.

"Give me a couple of days." Florence wiped sticky hands on her apron. "I'll pretend I found his badge or something and that I'm looking to give it back. See what I can turn up."

That's the only benefit of being a Mower. Everyone thinks they're dumb and harmless. They'll say things around a Mower they'd never dare tell a Regulator.

Two days later, Florence was back at the Calamari stand. I bought her a bag and we sat down.

"Elvis Presley hadn't been in the job for very long." She shovelled the food into her mouth. "He was only fourteen."

A year younger than me. I'd figured as much.

"He had a beat in District Seven. Did his job competently but wasn't flashy. Never drew attention to himself." She grinned. "Kinda the opposite of you."

"Yeah, yeah. Just give me the story."

"I found out he used to make visits to an old man called Robert Ropemaker Lee, but I can't see any connection they could have. Lee lives in the Fifth Ring with his granddaughter, Jane Austen. Her parents died in a fishing accident."

"Promising." I stroked my chin. I'm trying to grow a beard like Dad, but nothing is happening so far. "I'll pay him a visit."

"Can I come?"

"No." I shook my head. "I don't want you to see this."

"What are you going to do?" Florence put her hand on my arm. "He's probably just a harmless old guy."

"Then he'll be safe, won't he? My whole career is at stake."

"At least you have a career," Florence pouted. "My job is literally watching grass grow."

I looked at her cracked and grimy nails, clutching the bag of squid.

"You just stay put," I warned. "I don't need you getting in the way or trying to be my conscience."

"What if I refuse? You'll arrest me?"

"If I thought it would get my life back," I said coldly. "I'd chop you up and feed you to the fish."

"You sure know how to sweet talk a girl," Florence sniggered.

She obviously thought I was joking.

-9-

I peered in Robert Lee's window, keeping low. He was a hefty guy with sinewy hands and muscular arms covered in home-made tattoos. Still, he looked awfully old. Certainly not a problem for a Regulator, even a lone one.

Nor was his company.

I counted five kids, sitting attentively on kegs and coils of rope scattered around his workshop. They were all a little younger than me, holding flat slabs of slate and pieces of chalk. An unregulated school, huh? Promising.

It wasn't actually illegal but it *was* unusual and definitely frowned upon. Who knew what anti-Council nonsense Lee was filling their heads with? He might even be preparing them as future Goners. The problem was, I couldn't hear what he was saying through the glass.

I thought about waiting until everyone had gone, then searching the place, but there was a tatty bed in the corner of the hut. Lee obviously lived in his workshop, as many Citizens had to do.

That left the direct approach. Scare the hell out of them.

I unfastened the clip on my baton and tried the door. To my surprise it was unlocked, so I strode right in. The kids gasped when they saw the Regulator jacket and one or two quickly hid their writing implements.

"All right you lot," I said in my most authoritative voice. "I want everybody's name. If you lie, I'll know and I'll arrest you. Got it?"

"Why you wanna to know their names?" Robert Lee sat down on the edge of a bench and folded his burly arms. He didn't look particularly put out. "We just havin a little discussion group. Nothin wrong with that."

It was my turn to look shocked. *Nobody* talked to a Regulator that way.

"Here's how it works, old man." I snatched the writing apparatus from the smallest child. "I ask and they answer. Honestly and straight away."

I pointed the chalk round the room, memorising the faces.

"All your names. Now."

"Winston Fisher Churchill." Short black kid. A bit overweight.

"Napoleon Mechanic Bonaparte." This one was tiny with a wiry athletic frame.

"Marylin Fruitseller Monroe." Definitely the youngest. She immediately burst into tears.

"Shut up," I snapped. "You're co-operating, so there's nothing to get upset about."

I glanced at Robert Lee. His jaw was clenched but, wisely, he kept quiet.

"George Military Custer." Jeez. A Soldier's kid. Custer had platinum blonde hair and a chiselled jaw, which he stuck out defiantly.

"Jane Ropemaker Austen." This one was tall and athletic with long red hair. She looked me straight in the eye, her voice calm and measured. She was obviously Robert Lee's granddaughter.

I wrote down each name.

"Has this old man been telling you anything... eh… bad about the island or our Town Council?"

The children shook their heads. All except Jane Austen, who was still glaring at me with her bright green eyes. I could see now that she was my age, and her accusing gaze was unsettling.

"You won't get into trouble." I adopted a softer tone. "Not if you keep things above board."

The children looked at the floor, though Custer and Austen risked a hate filled glance at me.

"Bully boy. I been telling these littles *lotsa* bad things." Robert Lee eased himself off the workbench and fetched a bottle of potato hooch. "You got their names, so why not let em trot off? I'll happily give you the same lesson."

He was certainly a cool customer. I considered his request. After all, it was the organ grinder I wanted. Not the monkeys.

"All right. You troublemakers get out." I jerked a thumb over my shoulder. "It's getting dark, anyway. Get home and stay there."

They practically ran for the door. All except Jane Austen.

"I live here, dummy."

"Go stay with friends." Robert Lee waved the girl away. "I'll be fine."

"You sure?" she hesitated. "This guy seems like a prize dope."

"*Excuse* me..." I began. But her grandfather nodded. Jane Austen curled her lip into a disdainful sneer and left, throwing me a final look of contempt.

Then we were alone.

"You want a snifter?" Robert Lee poured the hooch into a battered tin mug. "It'll put hairs on your chin. Stop you lookin like a child tryin to do a man's job."

"I'm underage. It's illegal to offer me booze."

"So throw me in the clinky." Lee took a long gulp and punched his chest. "I ain't done nothin you can prove. Not fore the Council take away you shiny fizz stick an send you to the Tower."

I gave a start. How could a *Ropemaker* have gotten that kind of information? But I pressed on.

"You ever have a Regulator by the name of Elvis Presley in your little discussion group?"

"You must think so, or you wouldn't be here." Robert Lee went back to the bench and folded his arms again. "Why doncha come right out an ask what you wanna know?"

Why not?

"Did you ever... talk about anything that would make Presley decide to desert?"

"Probably."

Huh? Was this guy *looking* to get himself executed?

"What exactly did you say?"

Robert Ropemaker Lee gave a sly smile.

"I tole him bout the fish."

"What's to tell?" I tried to act blasé. "They smell, they're wriggly and they're all around us."

"Here's your dilemma." The old man poured himself another large shot. "If you wanna find out what he knew, take yourself a seat an open your ears." He raised a bushy white eyebrow. "Open your mind too."

A clever move. Voluntarily listening to dissent was treason, but I didn't have a lot of options. Besides, there was only him and me in the room. And who would take the word of a Ropemaker over a Regulator?

I might have thought that through a bit more.

"I'm going to show you somethin." Lee went to a ramshackle cupboard and pulled out a pair of books.

What the…? I'd never even seen *one* book before.

"Where did you get those?"

"They were smuggled onto the island when it was founded." Lee slammed a hefty tome on the barrel in front of me. "I happened to come across em."

The Encyclopaedia of Marine Life.

"Have a look through," he continued. "It's got pretty pictures if your reading skills aint too hot."

"I can read fine." Ignoring the jibe, I flicked through the book. It was illustrated with photographs of fish, all with names I'd never heard before. Mackerel. Cod. Tuna. Marlin. Haddock. Didn't recognise the pictures either.

"Now look at the date this was written," Lee said. "It's at the beginnin."

I did. The encyclopaedia was published two years before New Hebrides was founded.

"I've never seen any of these in the sea. Is this book made up?"

"Oh, sure," Robert Lee replied scathingly. "It's an encyclopaedia of imaginary fish."

"Then they must have died out."

"In less than two hunnert years?" He rolled his eyes. "That's not how evolution works. S'not like there's any wheat underwater to kill em off."

"What's evolution?"

Lee sighed and placed the other volume in front of me. It was big and brightly coloured and I struggled with the title.

The Big Bumper Anthology of Prehistoric Creatures.

"It's for kids," Lee grinned. "Even you should be able to unnerstand it."

"I'm the one holding the stunner, wrinkles." I opened the book. "Don't forget that."

And right there was a drawing of a Humble Squid. Only it was called *Tusoteuthis*, a member of the Teuthid Family, according to the text.

"Didn't know that Squids *had* families," I joked. "You think they hold tentacles when they go hunting humans?"

"You'd be the expert on huntin humans," Lee shot back. "Just keep lookin at the pictures, genius."

I began to flick through. In this volume, there *were* creatures I recognised. More types of squid and also Monster Fish that we land using the rigs. But I had never heard them called by these names before.

Brachauchenius. Bonnericthy. Xiphactinus.

"This is why I hate reading," I complained. "Monster Fish describes these horrors just fine. Why the big words?"

"Never mind that. Look at the dates *they* became extinct." Robert Lee stabbed a stubby digit at the page. "You *do* know what extinct means?"

"Of course. And *you'll* be extinct if you keep disrespecting me."

I put my finger under the words, faintly embarrassed that I had to do so.

According to the book, all these sea creatures died out during the Cretaceous period. Which ended 65 million years ago.

I looked up, furrowing my brow.

"This can't be right," I stammered. "You must have changed the pages somehow."

"Oh sure. I got my own printing press at the back o the workshop." Robert Lee pulled the book away from me. "Right next to my space rocket."

"How can there be prehistoric fish off the shore of New Hebrides?"

"Got no idea." Lee put the put the books back in the cupboard. "But I'll bet the Town Council do."

The Town Council! For a moment I had forgotten why I was here.

"Have you got any other stuff?" I asked casually.

"I scraped together this an that." Robert Lee shrugged. "It's been my life. Collectin things that everyone else forgot."

Suddenly he looked sad.

"Somebody has to."

I felt sorry for him. I really did. But this guy, no matter how good his intentions, was inspiring Goners. This was what I had hoped for. Turning him in, along with his stash, would redeem me.

"I apologise, old man." I pulled out my baton. "I have to place you under arrest."

"I figgered." Robert Lee nodded. "But it might not be as easy as you think."

"Don't try to threaten..." I began. Then I heard a click behind me.

I spun round, raising the stunner.

My friend, Florence Mower Nightingale, was pointing a pistol at my head.

-Part 2-

A l a n   C a r v e r

The idea that the laws of nature can vary must be taken seriously.

New Scientist Magazine

-10-

That's the way it is with people, I suppose. You try and help them and all you get is hurt.

"This isn't what it looks like," I said, raising my hands.

"This is exactly what it looks like," Robert Lee chipped in. He was right of course, but I wasn't giving up without a fight.

"Florence, you can't point a gun at a Regulator. You just... can't."

I lowered my baton slowly.

"Where did you *get* a gun?"

"I told you." Lee piped up again. "I collect stuff."

"See?" I said reasonably. "He's not some harmless old wrinkly. He's trying to get kids to desert. I have to turn him in."

"Did you show John the photograph?" Florence asked Lee.

"Wait a minute!" I stuttered. "You're working *with* him?"

I should have known. Too many coincidences. The mugging in the alley throwing us together. An ordinary kid wanting to hang out with a Regulator.

Florence having the perfect job to go snooping for me.

I'd been set up.

"I'm sorry, John." The pistol never wavered. "This thing is bigger than both of us."

"Florence was bettin you wouldn't turn her in for breakin curfew," Lee strolled over and gently took the baton from my hand. "She had faith in your good nature."

"She's sorely testing it now."

"All I want you to do is listen to what Mr Lee has to say." Florence waved me to a wooden chair with the barrel of her gun. "If you don't want to help after that, arrest us. We won't resist."

I was still seething but playing along seemed the best way out of this sorry situation.

"All right." I sat down and scowled at them. "I'm listening."

"When I was a little un myself," Lee began. "The storm warnin systems worked. There were lights on all night. The processing plants ran round the clock. Plastic and metal products wasn't rationed."

"Yeah, yeah," I sulked, mimicking his rustic accent. "The good ole days."

"New Hebrides is runnin out of power and materials." Lee sat opposite me, twirling the baton between his fingers. "Runnin out fast, I reckon."

"Everyone knows we're going through hard times," I conceded. "But what are we supposed to do about it?"

"Get off the island," Florence said. "Before it descends into chaos and everyone starves to death."

"Aw, not this again," I groaned. "There's no place to run. If there was, the Council would put the whole population on boats and head there."

"A sound argument but it's wrong." Robert Lee bent over and pulled up a floorboard. "Of all the things I've collected over the years, two are more precious to me than my own life."

He pulled out a plastic water bottle, standard New Hebrides issue, and passed it to me.

"I'm not thirsty."

"Put your fingers inside."

I did so and pulled out a tiny scrap of cloth.

"This was given to me a few years ago." Lee sat back and pulled at his white beard. "It got washed up on the shore. See what's written on it."

I did. The writing was tiny but filled the little scrap.

There is land in the east. No wheat. It's v dangerous but I'm still alive.

"This is some nut on the island playing a practical joke!" I yelled. "Are you both completely insane?"

"I didn't think you official types would be up for much tomfoolery." Lee chided. "Check out the material."

Though I had no idea what tomfoolery meant, I scrutinized the scrap of cloth. It was finely woven and blood red, just like my own uniform.

It had been torn from a Regulator's jacket.

"New Hebrides will probably survive a few more years, but there are a bunch o adults on the island who don want their kids to be around when it finally goes down the tubes." Lee took the bottle back. "Of course, the boffins in the tech labs may still find a way to destroy the wheat, but plenty of us don't believe that's gonna happen in time."

"Are you saying this is a movement? Not just a handful of kids?" Suddenly I was very interested. If I could thwart an entire revolution, I could probably skip the exam and go straight to being an Inspector. Imagine how proud Dad would be!

"I'm sayin there's plenty people willin to desert," Lee replied vehemently. "But they're too scared to make that final move. They need a leader."

"And that would be you?" I snorted.

"Me?" Lee cackled. "I lived here all my life an, despite what you might think, I'm proud o this place. I aint never leavin."

He leaned over and patted me on the knee.

"The leader they need is *you*."

<h1 style="text-align:center">-11-</h1>

I couldn't believe my ears. Between them, these guys had lied, betrayed me, preached treason and held me prisoner at gunpoint. Now my captors wanted me to lead them on a suicide mission or get arrested and executed trying.

They certainly had some nerve.

But I could use this to my advantage. Gain their trust. Once I got my baton back and Florence had put down her gun, I'd make a run for it and call in backup.

"Why would anyone want me to lead them?" I admit, I was genuinely puzzled. "I'm a Regulator, who doesn't believe there's anywhere to go."

I caught myself quickly.

"Not that you haven't raised some doubts in my mind, what with that message in a bottle."

"Power isn't the only thing running low in New Hebrides." Florence took up the story. "The DNA banks on the island are finite too. Obviously, the Town Council would use the catalogued samples first. But we think they've run out of those and are forced to utilize Unidentifieds that were collected in the last days."

"What makes you think that?"

"More and more kids seem to be doing jobs they're not really suited for."

"Like you, I suppose?" I could hardly bring myself to look at her.

"Like me." Florence nodded. "And you."

"What?" I was completely taken aback. "I'm a pretty good Regulator, I'll have you know."

"You was trained since birth, that's all." Robert Lee began rummaging in the hole in the floor again. "But then, there's probably nuthin you couldn't do if you put you mind to it."

"Thank you very much," I said. "I *am* a bit of a bulldog."

"If your job was collectin DNA, in the days when the world was fallin apart." Lee's arm had disappeared up to his shoulder. "What's the one sample you'd want over all others?"

That was a no brainer.

"Alan Carver," I replied without hesitation. "But he was killed in the Great Chaos."

"It don mean his DNA weren't collected." Lee withdrew his arm, clutching a sheet of yellowed paper. "Maybe it just wasn't identified."

Alan Carver ending up an Unidentified? That would certainly be a cruel joke but I supposed it *was* possible. He was a reclusive man, who used a spokeswoman to make all his announcements and wouldn't allow his picture to be taken. And, though he was rich, he didn't really become a legend until after he was dead.

"*We've* identified him." Lee unfolded the battered square and handed it to me. "This is called a newspaper. They used to print 'em to tell people what was goin on in their neck o the woods. It's the most important thing I own."

At the top of the sheet was a name and date.

Akron Weekly: 4ᵗʰ June 1974

Akron. I recalled that was Alan Carver's home town, somewhere in what was called USA.

Underneath was a headline.

Local Teen Stands Up To Vicious Street Gang.

There was a blurb below about how a fifteen-year-old had intervened in a street mugging on Victoria Street, Akron, saving a businessman from being robbed.

The boy's name was Alan Carver.

"Now, don't that just sound like the kind o selfless act the hero of New Hebrides would attempt?" Lee asked.

But I wasn't listening. I was too busy trying to get my head round the accompanying photograph.

"Far as I know, nobody ever seed a snapshot o Carver as a child," Lee continued. "But he'd be fifteen in 1974."

The Ropemaker gave a throaty laugh and winked at Florence.

"That's him, all right."

I stared at the picture again.

Alan Carver was thinner than me and had a longer hair. He was wearing a high-necked black top under some kind of shiny matching jacket and had a bloody cut on his forehead.

Apart from that, his face was identical to mine. Not similar. *Identical.*

"You want to know why people will follow you?" Florence finally put down the gun. "Why *I'll* follow you?"

"No!" I said vehemently. "This can't be right!"

"Looks like Alan Carver's DNA was collected, after all." Lee took the paper from my lifeless fingers and folded it carefully. "Just never recognized… until now."

He sat back and regarded me with wonder.

"*You're* Alan Carver." he grinned.

"Saviour o the human race."

-12-

My head was spinning. This couldn't be right. This *couldn't* be right.

"I'm not a genius," I blurted, though it pained me to say so. "I don't know anything about science."

"Course not," Lee tisked. "You never been taught anythin but runnin round and whackin people with your boom stick." He tossed the baton to me. "Which you can now have back."

"Your choice." Florence bit her finger nervously. "You can lead us or you can turn us in."

"Fore you make that decision, there's somethin you might like to think about." Lee cautioned. "If the Town Council found out who you was, they'd drag you to their labs an you'd never come out. If anyone could figger out how to destroy the wheat, it'd be you. They'd cut you into slices and use every bit of your DNA to try and clone more Alan Carvers."

"They don't know how to do that," I objected. "Or else they'd just use DNA samples from the existing population to make more people."

"And you say you aint no scientist!" Lee thumped the bench. Then his face became serious. "I reckon they'd try anyhow. You're too much of a prize not to give it a go."

They'd outmanoeuvred me again.

"Can I have time to think?" I went to the window and looked out. "This is a lot to take in."

"Course. You're our potential leader."

I couldn't decide what to do. If I arrested Lee and Florence now, they'd tell the Town Council who I was and I'd end up human Sushi. I didn't see how things could get any worse.

I scratched my temple with the baton, trying to get my thoughts in order. My reflection repeated the action, staring miserably back at me from the dark pane.

Dark pane.

There had been a light outside when I was spying on Robert Lee. Now it was extinguished, even though curfew wasn't for another hour.

I remembered what I'd told Lee's terrified audience.

You won't get into trouble. Not if you tell the truth.

One of them obviously *had* told the truth. And gone straight to the authorities with it.

That pretty much decided things for me. I'd been sitting here for over an hour listening to the damned King of the Dissidents and his sidekick.

Nobody would believe Lee had forced me, not when I was standing in a lit window holding my baton. I had no choice.

"One of your kids has turned us in," I said quietly. "Put the lights out and get me a gun."

Lee moved fast for a man his age. Within seconds he had extinguished all the candles and the room was plunged into darkness. I felt Florence's pistol being pressed into my hand and her soft breath at my ear.

"Sorry, John," she whispered. "We'll try and get you out of here."

I crouched below the window and peered over the sill, letting my eyes adjust to the darkness. Soon I could see figures flitting from shack to shack, their hands held together, as if in prayer.

But I knew that stance.

They weren't praying, they were holding blasters.

Not Regulators, then. Those were armed Lawmen.

I smashed the window with my baton and fired a warning round over their heads. The figures ducked behind the nearest cover and began shooting back.

The rest of the glass exploded inwards, covering me in glittering shards, as bullets thudded into the far wall. Behind me, I could hear Robert Lee pulling up more floorboards. Florence joined me, carrying a pump shotgun.

"What the…?" My eyes widened. "Is this a workshop or an armoury?"

"Bit of both." She stood quickly and blasted a round into the night. The ejected cartridge bounced off my head and I gave a resigned sigh.

The Lawmen returned fire even more vehemently.

"Down here!"

I glanced over my shoulder. Enough floorboards had been removed to reveal an open trapdoor underneath. Lee squeezed his bulk through the gap. Florence and I scooted across the floor using our elbows and dived headfirst into the hole after him. While we picked ourselves up, Lee adjusted what looked like a timer on a couple of grey canisters and tossed them into the room. Then he pulled the trapdoor shut and lit a rusty paraffin lamp.

The shelter was small but extremely well stocked. Shelves lined the walls, covered in cans of food, weapons and objects from the past that I didn't remotely recognise. And there were more books. Lots more books.

It looked like Robert Lee had been running his operation for a very long time.

He pulled the newspaper clipping from inside his jacket and thrust it into the lamp, flinching as he watched the most vital thing he'd ever owned curl into oblivion.

"Only the kids I trust most know bout the picture," he explained. "You might get executed, but I won't see you used as an experiment."

"That's very comforting." I began examining the walls. "But I've no intention of getting arrested. Where's the escape tunnel?"

"Whaddya think I am? A mole?" Lee pulled a rifle from the wall. "There aint no scape tunnel."

"You *trapped* us down here?" I shouted. "What kind of cretin builds an escape hatch he can't use to *escape*?"

As if on cue, we heard the front door splinter and the sound of boots thudding into the room above us. Lee waved at me to keep quiet. He fetched a couple of strange masks from a shelf, all glass eyepieces and blunt snouts.

"Get ready," he whispered. "5… 4… 3… 2… 1…"

There was a loud *whump* from above. Then the sound of coughing and bodies hitting the floor.

"What were those canisters you threw up there?"

"S'called tear gas." Lee fastened one of the masks on Florence so that she looked like some kind of bug. "They was used to control riots durin the Great Chaos. Won do the Lawmen any long-term harm but I bet they aint in the mood for a scrap no more."

"Where's yours?" I pulled on my mask and tightened the straps.

"Only got two." Shouldering the rifle, Lee tied a handkerchief over his face and pushed open the hatch. Tendrils of grey smoke floated down.

Arming himself with two more canisters, he wriggled into the workshop, flung them out of the broken front door and pulled Florence and me after him. There were two more *whumps* outside and panicked shouting.

Go, the old man motioned, shoving us towards the door.

Florence led the way since she knew the area better than me. We raced into a side alley, then another, then another. We could hear the crack of Lee's rifle and flashes lit the night air as the Lawmen, retreating beyond the reach of the gas, began shooting back.

Frightened faces peered from doorways as we sprinted to safety. The shacks were crowded together and laced with dozens of tiny passageways. We twisted and turned, panting breath fogging the masks. At full tilt, we rounded a corner and almost ran into an Inspector, standing with his back to us.

As he turned around, Florence raised her shotgun.

"No!" I slammed the barrel up and the gun discharged into the sky.

The officer stopped, pistol pointed at my chest. I reached up and pulled off my mask. Florence followed suit.

"Don't shoot," I implored. "It's me."

"*John*?"

It was hard to describe the look on my father's face. Horror didn't even begin to cover it.

"Dad…" I began. "This is going to be a little difficult to explain."

"You *think*?" He looked around quickly and lowered his gun. "Get out of here. Quickly."

But it was too late. We could hear footsteps behind us and a pair of armed Lawmen emerged from the gloom.

My father's face twitched as he fought to control his emotions. He raised his gun again.

"It's all right boys," he shouted. "They've surrendered to me."

"Well done, Inspector." One of the men saluted him. "We'll take it from here."

"That's all right," dad said calmly. "I can escort them to the station. It's my collar."

"Orders are orders, Sir." An officer took me by the arm. "These two are dangerous terrorists and we can't let them out of our sight."

Dad nodded. But I could see his trigger finger tightening as he inched the pistol away from me and towards my captors.

I caught his eye and shook my head.

My father took a deep breath. A tear slid down his cheek. Then he holstered his firearm and walked away, back ramrod straight.

He didn't look back.

-13-

The courtroom was white and bare, with an antique wooden desk and high-backed chair lurking at one end. Above that, the symbol of New Hebrides was stencilled on the wall - a pair of dice on a string. There were also two armed guards at the door who studiously avoided looking in my direction.

I presumed the smaller chair in the middle of the room was for me, but I didn't know if I was supposed to sit on it yet. So I stood and waited.

A thin, bald man entered. He was wearing the dark green robes of a Town Council official.

"Be seated, boy," he said. "I'm Douglas Judge Macarthur." He eased himself behind the desk. "Name?"

"John Regulator Wayne, Sir." Like he didn't already have *that* information.

"You'll be happy to learn nobody was killed yesterday," the Judge continued. "Except for your mentor, Robert Ropemaker Lee."

I was shocked for a second but quickly recovered my composure. I suppose I'd half expected

91

the news. The last time I saw Lee he was popping his gun at anything that moved.

"He wasn't my mentor," I replied honestly. "I'd never met him before last night."

Macarthur raised an eyebrow.

"Sir. May I see my father?"

"No."

"He'll vouch that I wasn't part of any plot to desert," I persisted. "I was only there to trap Lee, so the Town Council wouldn't send me to the Towers."

"That worked out well for you, didn't it?"

I'd mentally prepared for all sorts of official responses to my actions. Anger. Disappointment. Even torture.

I *wasn't* expecting sarcasm.

"If you'd only listen to what I have to say, Sir, I'm sure I can convince you."

"I don't really care if you're telling the truth." The Judge looked down at the notes on his desk. "A dozen Lawmen and at least twenty Citizens saw you battle your way out of the Ropemaker's house. The Council have to assure them you'll be appropriately punished."

"So that's it?" I felt tears sting my eyes. "I'm just going to be executed? No attempt to hear my side of the story?"

"Calm yourself, lad." The Judge dismissed my plea with a wave of his bony hand. "Nobody on this island has ever been executed. We're not the Spanish Inquisition."

"But… I… I mean…. *What?*"

"It's true, if someone breaks the law, the Town Council sentences them to death." Macarthur tapped his fingers together. "It puts the fear of God into the population and, with our rigid social structure, that's necessary to maintain order. But we don't actually kill anyone."

I felt a great wave of relief wash over me, quickly followed by a stab of suspicion.

"So what *do* you do with people who break the law?"

"We exile the most extreme lawbreakers and *all* Goners to the east." The judge licked his fingers and rifled through the papers on his desk. "With a strict warning that they *will* be killed if they ever try to return." He scratched his cheek. "Though I'm fairly sure it's impossible to get back, in any case."

"You mean there really *is* habitable land out there?" My head was whirling.

"Depends on what you mean by habitable." Macarthur got up and edged round the desk, a small brown folder in his hand. "I was going to explain the situation but you can read and you seem bright enough."

He reached me and handed over the folder.

"Take a look. This was written during the last days of the Great Chaos."

I opened the folder. Inside were a few sheets of creased paper.

Report on the Sixth Ring
by Dr Evan Williams

When Alan Carver and his team at Atlantic City were declared dead, I took over as Head of Scientific Research at New Hebrides.

I had a hard decision to make.

Carver had proved the irradiation machines would keep the Golden Plague at bay, even though we still had no cure for the wheat infestation. The island was already self-sufficient and I calculated it could remain so for well over a century. We'd collected enough human genetic samples to replenish New Hebrides' population for that amount of time and stored animal DNA to restock the mainland once we had figured out how to overcome the plague.

My immediate problem was the survivors who were still out there. The human race was dying, but it hadn't gone yet. Our military had picked up transmissions as far away as China and Newfoundland, where populations were grimly clinging on. And they knew about our island sanctuary.

At first, the foreign heads of state begged to be allowed to move here, but we simply had no room. So they threatened us with destruction if we didn't comply.

New Hebrides had firepower but not enough to repel a serious invasion and I couldn't take the chance that some regime with nuclear capability would annihilate us just to be petty.

Though the Sixth Ring wasn't a weapon, I suspected we could use it to defend ourselves. A risky move, for I only had Carver's notes to go on. It was his baby, after all.

He had ordered the Sixth Ring built round the island before the Golden Plague struck. It was a variation on existing matter colliders like the Large Hadron in Switzerland – only much bigger. The Foundation used the 300-mile tube in experiments - accelerating sub-atomic particles to almost light speed, then smashing them together, to see what would happen.

In initial tests, they got results that shouldn't have been possible. The collisions pushed random particles to a velocity that was actually equal to light. I won't go into the technical details but, in essence, if you achieve that speed with anything other than light, you can feasibly warp time.

Then, inexplicably, Carver shut the Ring down. At the time, I didn't know why.

So I started it up again.

I thought I had no choice. I took a gamble.

I'm sorry.

This was all mumbo jumbo to me. I had to remind myself that I *was* Alan Carver and should be able to understand. But, even if I couldn't comprehend Dr William's 'technical details', the phrase *you could feasibly warp time* was plain enough.

I kept reading.

I modified the Ring myself, using Carver's formulae, for I believed it could be used to displace New Hebrides in time.

The idea was beautifully simple. Keep the Ring on long enough to jump the island forward a few decades. Then we could concentrate on the problem of killing the wheat without fear of attack and repopulate a globe now entirely devoid of humanity. To my horror, the experiment didn't work the way I'd hoped.

Instead, the Sixth Ring somehow jumbled up time itself. Not a very scientific explanation, I know, but it's the best way I can describe it. And I have a Nobel Prize.

If you leave the island and sail west, you reach the American mainland. We sent scouting parties out and, judging by the state of the ruins we found, New Hebrides had indeed leapt about fifty years into the future. The wheat was still thriving but all other life, as I'd predicted, was gone.

So far, so good. If you can call the end of the world a positive result.

Then we sent planes east and got the shock of our lives. In that direction, we'd somehow jumped back in time. Way back.

A long, long way back.

Hundreds of millions of years, in fact.

That was unexpected.

"Millions of years?" My jaw dropped. "You have *got* to be joking."

"Hard to take, I know." The judge gave a thin smile. "But do I look like the kind of man who fools around?"

He didn't. I moved my fingers under the rest of the words, too engrossed to be embarrassed.

What we found contravened every law of physics, but the proof was incontrovertible. The sea to the east was now inhabited by prehistoric marine life and our planes took pictures of dinosaurs on the mainland. We sent out scouting parties but they never came back. I couldn't afford to lose any more people, so I stopped all eastern exploration.

There was only one conclusion I could come to.

Travelling west from the island, it's the late 21st century and I predict it stays that way right round the planet. Nothing but wheat and no chance of survival, until we can figure out how to kill it.

Travelling east, however, it's the Mesozoic Era, judging by the description of the monsters our planes spotted.

I went over my calculations again and eventually came up with a theory that defied belief. Yet I'm sure it's correct.

In the east, time and space have become fused in a completely new way. I think that if you continue to head in that direction, you'll begin moving forward in time. If you managed to circumnavigate the globe, you'd actually end up back at the point where the Sixth Ring was switched on.

I doubt anyone could make it, though, and it wouldn't matter much if they did.

They'd just come back to where they started.

I got up and placed the folder back on James Judge Macarthur's desk. It was probably a breach of protocol, but I was too stunned to care.

"So you exile people who break the law to the east," I said. "And I bet you give Goners a good chance of escaping, so they'll head the same way."

"Very astute." Macarthur slid the folder into a drawer. "We can't afford to keep troublemakers on the island, spreading their doubts and dissent, but we're not prepared to descend into savagery and kill them. Better they take their chances in the distant past."

"It doesn't sound like they stand much of a chance."

"You'll find that out for yourself." The judge waved me back to my chair.

"You're going with the next batch."

<h1 style="text-align:center">-14-</h1>

My fate was sealed. There was no point in appealing to Macarthur's good nature, as he obviously didn't have one.

I figured I may as well speak my mind.

"Dr William's report states that New Hebrides was only designed to be self-sufficient for a century or so," I pointed out. "We've been here longer than that."

"True."

"Robert Lee told me the island is running out of power, has exhausted its DNA reserves and you still haven't found a way to destroy the wheat." I took a deep breath. "We're on our last legs, aren't we?"

"I'm not here for a debate," Macarthur replied testily. "This is your trial and it's over."

"You got something better to do?" I retorted. "Except go home and wait for your carefully preserved way of life to fall to pieces."

Douglas Judge Macarthur looked *extremely* put out by that statement. I could see he wasn't used to being stood up to.

But what did I have to lose? I was the reincarnation of Alan Carver, Saviour of New Hebrides, and I wasn't going to accept his ruling without having my say.

"We'll find a way to kill the wheat," the official said defensively. "Our top scientists are working round the clock."

"Round the clock? They've been trying for well over a century without any success." It was my turn to give a dismissive wave and I took great satisfaction in the sour look it prompted. "Yet there's another solution staring you in the face."

"And what might that be?"

I took a wild guess.

"I'm assuming the Town Council kept the best DNA samples to repopulate the west, even though that's looking increasingly unlikely."

"As a matter of fact, we have," Macarthur nodded. "I must say, you're smarter than the average Regulator."

"Tell me about it. I was hoping to make Inspector one day."

"If you have a point, get to it."

"Why not resurrect those last DNA samples and take the whole population of New Hebrides *east*?" The room was windowless so I gestured vaguely in the direction I thought east might be. "We have weapons. We know how to make the best of meagre resources. And there's no wheat in the distant past, so you wouldn't have to irradiate the new kids. We could start a colony. We could *survive*."

"I admire your confidence, but plenty of others have come up with that idea." The judge rested his head wearily on one hand. "We do have some bona fide geniuses working in our labs, you know."

I was tempted to announce that none of them could hold a candle to me - but that would get me shuffled off to those very labs as a test subject. I'd rather take my chances with the dinosaurs.

"There are two reasons the population can't go east," Macarthur said wearily. "If we survived as a colony, there would be some fossil evidence of it in our own historical records. But there isn't. Humans and dinosaurs never co-existed."

He gave a heartfelt sigh.

"Which means, if we tried to make a go of it in the Mesozoic Era, we already *know* we'd fail."

That was a hard explanation to come to terms with, so I didn't try.

"What's the other reason?

"As far as we can calculate, it's approximately 2130, give or take a few years." The judge got up and paced the room, hands behind his back. "And the whole world is dead in 2130 except the population of this island."

He closed his eyes.

"So what happens if we abandon New Hebrides and take the entire population into the past?"

I thought for a while. Then it came to me like a hammer blow.

"There would be *nobody* left in 2130." I realised what a horrifying concept that presented. "The human race would have become extinct."

"Exactly." Douglas judge Macarthur shook his head miserably. "And that's not going to happen on my watch. We have to hang on to the bitter end, no matter how slim the chances of finding a cure for the Golden Plague."

The last words caught in his throat.

"In a way, you may be more fortunate than the rest of New Hebrides." He tried a reassuring smile but it didn't sit well on his sober face. "It's possible you could find an existing colony of exiles, one small enough never to have been discovered in fossil records. You might even live a full life with them, albeit one where you risk getting eaten every day."

"What if Dr William's theory is correct?" I was firing on all cylinders now. "What if I went east but didn't stop? What if I travelled right round the world, moving through time as well as space? Try to change what happened."

"You'd have wasted your time," Macarthur laughed bitterly. To my surprise, he came over and laid a hand on my shoulder.

"It's a nice thought. But if you try, you'll die. You *can't* change the past."

"Why not?"

"Because, if you had, we wouldn't *be* in this situation. It's called a paradox."

I could see how that made sense. Sort of.

Still… I'm a bit of a bulldog.

"I'm going to give it my best shot." I folded my arms. "This is my island and, despite the way you've treated me, I have to try and save it."

Macarthur withdrew his hand and looked at me for a long time.

"We're sending a combined Military, Naval and Scientific squad east tomorrow," he said finally. "We haven't done that for many years, because nobody ever returns. But there are certain minerals that we have run out of on New Hebrides. Minerals we simply can't reproduce here."

He pursed his thin lips.

"We're desperate, boy. The expedition *has* to come back with these resources, so they're better equipped than any previous scouting party. Heavily armoured and armed. Carrying the remnants of New Hebrides' serious technological hardware. It's our last chance."

"Why are you telling me this?"

"You and Lee's other protégés will go with them." The Judge patted my cheek. "You'll be left there, of course, but I'll instruct the soldiers to give you weapons and supplies. Then you'll, at least, have a chance."

"Thank you," I whispered.

"I'll let your father know what I've done, though it's a breach of procedure. He's an Inspector so I'll take a chance he'll stay quiet."

Macarthur signalled for the guards to open the door.

"You impressed me, son. If it's any consolation, I believe you never intended to desert."

"Nope. Not much."

"Sucks to be you, then."

So he *did* have a sense of humour. I just didn't find it funny.

"I'm going to go right round the world, mark my words." I put on my best game face and thumped my chest dramatically.

"I'm *going* to find a way to save the human race."

I might have thought that through a bit more.

-15-

The amphibious carrier ploughed through choppy seas, belching smoke from its diesel engine. I counted another four boats bobbing above the swells on either side of our craft.

The carriers were designed to travel on both water and land. They were boxy, open topped vehicles about fifteen feet long, with a folded down canvas top. A mounted gun turret at the prow was manned by a blue-capped Naval and the rest of the adult contingent consisted of three soldiers and a Scientist. I was a bit surprised by this since the carrier could hold a lot more people. We lawbreakers were jammed in the stern, getting a face full of salty water every time the craft crested a wave and sank into a trough.

I recognised my fellow felons the moment we boarded at dawn. Winston Fisher Churchill, Napoleon Mechanic Bonaparte, George Military Custer, Jane Ropemaker Austen and, of course, Florence.

No prizes for guessing who had turned us in. There was no sign of Marylin Fruitseller Monroe.

The Goners were scrunched on the port side, as far from me as they could get. Fine. I wasn't exactly in a talkative mood, watching the only home I had ever known recede into the mist.

Eventually, I curled into a ball and fell into a fitful sleep. It's a talent I have. The ability to take a nap in almost any circumstances.

When I woke, Florence was sitting next to me, looking a bit green.

"I just wanted to say sorry for getting you into this situation." She pulled a waterproof jacket tighter round her thin shoulders. "But you have to agree, we were right all along. There *was* a place to run to."

"Yeah. Straight into the jaws of some Stegosaurus."

"Stegosaurus eat plants."

"It's the only dinosaur name I remember." I turned my back on her. "Go away. I don't want to talk to you."

Florence flinched as if she had been slapped. Then she scuttled back to her group.

I sat in silence, thinking about my parents and trying not to cry. Eventually, I felt a tap on my arm.

"I told you, I don't…"

But it wasn't Florence by my side. It was Jane Austen.

"Pull yourself together, wimp," she hissed. "We're all in the same boat. Literally."

"You and your rebellious bunch ruined my life," I spat back.

"Really?" Her green eyes blazed. "We weren't to blame for you being sent to the Towers. You, on the other hand, are responsible for all of us being arrested and getting my grandfather killed."

Though I hated to admit it, she was spot on.

"We need to work together, if we're going to survive," she continued. "We've all got skills that will come in useful, but I reckon being able to fight will come tops. George Military Custer knows weapons but, obviously, doesn't have any. Grandad taught me how handle myself but I'm no Regulator."

"Exactly," I grunted. "I'll be fine on my own."

"You don't know what's out there and we do," Jane glowered. "That's the beauty of books. If you can't tell a Stegosaurus from a Tyrannosaurus, you're most likely to end up inside the latter."

Again, she was probably right.

"I doubt the rest of them will even speak to me," I huffed.

"Shrink your head. They were determined to get away, it just happened sooner than expected." She lowered her voice. "Besides, I've told them you're Alan Carver. They find it hard to believe, but they trust me. We'll help if you stop acting like a spoilt brat."

I thought about this for a moment. I *would* need allies until I adjusted to my new circumstances. If it didn't work out, I could always abandon them later.

"All right," I conceded. "I'll teach them how to fight if you tell me what we're actually going to be fighting."

"Ok. We have a deal, but I have to be honest about my intentions." Jane Austen hunched over as another wave burst across the prow. "I want to keep my friends safe so, for now, I'll obey you without question. But I loved my grandfather and he was the only family I had."

She lifted her head and the green eyes fastened on me.

"Once we've established a colony, however?" The girl pointed two fingers at me as she backed away.

"Alan Carver or not, I'm going to murder you."

I sat for a while, shivering and taking in this information. Austen's attitude was understandable, even though I'd ended up fighting on her grandad's side. I could see how she'd hold me partly responsible for his demise and I was genuinely sorry for her loss.

But I wasn't going to just roll over and take things lying down. If I had to kill *her* someday, I wouldn't hesitate.

It was time to man up, stop moping and concentrate on getting out of this mess.

I inched over to the huddled group.

"Let's start again." I cringed as I recalled how I'd handled our last encounter. "My name is John Regulator Wayne and I apologise for getting you exiled. Truly. Especially you, Florence."

Florence gave me a bright smile and suddenly I wasn't mad at her any more. In fact, I wasn't angry at all. I was better than a Regulator now. I was a leader and finally in control of my own destiny.

I might have thought that through a bit more.

"I need to know what we're going to be facing when the craft reaches land," I said decisively. "That way we can prepare to meet it head on. Or run away, which would seem to be the more sensible course of action."

"Alan?" Winston Fisher Churchill broke in. "Eh… I mean… John."

"You don't have to put your hand up."

"We're going to have problems long before we hit land."

"Really? You got something fishy to say?" I grinned at my own joke but nobody joined in.

"Fishermen are instructed to always cast our nets west of New Hebrides. If pickings are thin and we *do* have to go east, we use individual Coracles that sit light on the surface of the sea, so as not to draw the attention of squid or Monster Fish. We *never* go out as a fleet."

"I don't like the sound of this."

"You shouldn't. We're heading east in five heavy boats with powerful motors, all making a lot of noise."

"Which is a bad thing?" But I already knew the answer.

"It's possible sea creatures could mistake us for predators but I doubt it." Winston Churchill pulled at his lip. "They're going to think we're travelling together because we don't have any other defence."

"They're in for a shock then." I indicated the gun turret. "I bet that baby could blow anything apart."

"Yeah. But these aren't regular naval vessels. They've been modified to include heavy artillery. Problem is, the cannons don't point down in case they accidentally shoot a hole in the boat." Churchill curled his lip unhappily. "They could have thought that through a bit more."

Hey. That was *my* line.

"I haven't seen any squid," I said testily.

"That's probably because something more deadly has scared them away." The boy wiped spray from his eyes. "I doubt it's us."

"Captain!" I stood up. "Can you remove that big gun from its turret?"

"We can." At the wheel, a large man with a truly enormous stubbled chin turned and shouted back over the sound of the motors. "Why? You want to play with one?"

"This kid is a Fisherman," I waved my hand at Winston Churchill. "He thinks a Monster Fish may be about to attack us. Holding the gun manually would be our best defence."

"And why is that?" the Captain sneered.

"Cause you could actually aim it into the sodding water."

"I never seen a Monster Fish that could pierce any steel hull." The Captain gave a toothy grin. "A Humble Squid, on the other hand, can grab you from a boat like a Mower plucking a sheaf of wheat. The gun is for shooting off tentacles."

"We're in deep water now," Winston piped up timidly. "The Monster Fish will be bigger."

"Thanks for the tip." The Captain turned back to his steering. "But the day I take advice from some snot-nosed Goner will be…"

At that moment, the craft to our left rose out of the sea.

-16-

We only had seconds to take in what was happening. The terrified look on the faces of the crew. Our sister ship heading skywards with a huge grey form underneath. A rolling white eye and jaws so large they splintered the stern of the amphibious carrier like a child taking a bite from a tomato.

The fish submerged again, dragging the boat with it and leaving the screaming survivors bobbing in the water. One by one, they were sucked under the waves by smaller predators.

"It's a Megalodon!" Jane yelled. "A prehistoric shark. They grow up to 70 feet long."

That was more than three times the length of our boat.

To his credit, the Captain didn't question how the girl could possibly know this. He'd seen the size of the attacker himself.

"Get the gun off the casing!" he roared. "Point it into the water."

The crews were well-trained. While our occupants struggled to lift the cannon off its mount, the other craft veered away from each other, spreading out to present a less bunched target. The Captain made a snap decision.

"You Goners grab weapons," he commanded. "We'll need every man if we're going to get through this."

We dived into the arms locker and pulled out a variety of guns. Clutched the rail and scanned the waves looking for the shark, praying it wouldn't leap up and bite our heads off.

But we weren't the next victims.

The Megalodon rose out of the water, its mouth gaping, and the craft to our left sailed right into its maw. We fired volley after volley, to no effect, as it pulled the second boat under the waves.

Our crew had finally gotten the cannon off the mounting but it took three men to hold it. Even a landlubber like me could see it was going to be too slow to aim and fire unless we could predict where the shark would crop up next. The Captain realised it too.

"Point the cannon at boat number three," he barked. "If that beast attacks it, start shooting."

He was willing to sacrifice his own men, but I understood his dilemma. If we didn't take drastic action none of the expedition was going to reach dry land.

But boat four, the farthest away, was the next casualty. The Megalodon leapt out of the water, and brought its entire weight down on the craft, breaking it in two.

"All right, I'm willing to listen to any suggestions," the Captain bellowed. "Even from you kids."

"Do we have explosives?" Jane shouted back.

"Tubes of Nitro Glycerine." A Scientist was cowering near the prow. "They're for blasting rock to get at mineral samples."

"Are they in waterproof containers?"

"Of course. We're in a boat."

"We can tie them in a tarpaulin and use the whole thing as a depth charge." Florence joined in. "It's how ships used to destroy submarines in the old days."

"I told you. We need them to collect minerals!"

"Do what the girl says," the Captain countermanded. "Or we won't be collecting anything except angel wings."

The soldiers began frantically pulling out the packages and piling them into a tarpaulin.

"Careful!" the scientist threw his arms over his head. "Treat those too roughly and we'll be blown sky high."

The Captain got on the radio to boat number four and it drew closer until we could see the tense faces of its occupants. They too had unhooked their big gun. We had ours pointed at them. They had theirs pointed at us, waiting to see who would be attacked next. Only one ship was going to survive the onslaught and we both knew it.

A giant fin, the size of a sail, broke the surface two hundred yards away and headed straight for us.

"Get those explosives over the side now! Then turn hard astern and get us out of here!"

The Navals bundled the bulky tarp over the side where it bobbed on the water, slowly sinking.

We were moving away at top speed but the Megalodon halved the distance between it and us in seconds, its giant fin slicing through the choppy water like a razor.

"Fire on my command and, for God sake, don't miss."

The dorsal fin passed the tarpaulin, the wake almost plunging it completely under. The shark sensed this was a mere distraction and we were the real quarry. I almost admired its determination.

"Fire!" the Captain screamed.

We poured a volley of lead at the spot, just under the water, where we had last seen the tarp. Then there was a deafening boom as the cannon went off and the Soldiers holding it were flung onto their backs by the recoil.

But the next explosion was in a different league. The Nitro-Glycerine packages in the tarp erupted in a chain reaction sending a wall of water fifty feet in the air. Chunks of mangled shark splattered onto the deck as our boat rocked violently from side to side, throwing us around like dice in a cup. I hauled myself up and peered over the side of the craft at the bloody swells.

The other boat was gone.

The brunt of the explosion had been absorbed by the sea but our sister craft has simply been too close. It had vanished under the wall of water.

We were alone.

"Well done, you lot." The Captain looked over his shoulder at us. "Nice work."

He took several deep breaths and gripped the wheel with white knuckles.

"We are now officially the meanest thing in this ocean," he grunted. "Let's hope we can repeat the trick when we hit land."

"Shouldn't we say something before we go?" one of the Navals removed his hat. "About the others?"

"Say goodbye." The Captain gunned the boat to life. "I'm not inclined to hang around for more than that."

And we headed east at maximum speed.

-Part 3-

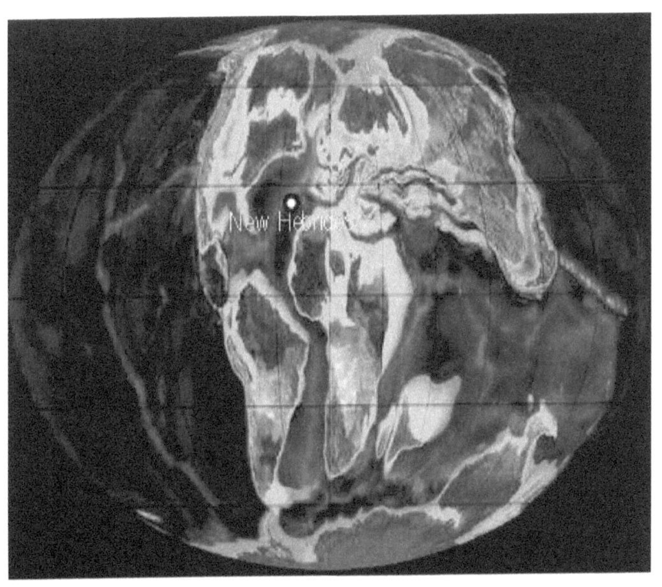

*Map of the Earth during the Jurassic Period
of the Mesozoic Era*

-17-

Nobody had talked for hours. We were too busy staring at the water in case another fin appeared.

"Where exactly are we?" I asked the Captain. "I mean… *when* are we?"

I still couldn't get to grips with that.

Now that we had proved our worth, the Captain seemed willing to talk to us. Besides, the rest of his crew were still mourning the loss of their comrades.

"If our Scientists back home are right, we're in the Jurassic Period of the Mesozoic Era."

"No idea what you just said," I frowned. "Pretend you're explaining it to a complete idiot."

"We're in monster paradise, you complete idiot."

I suppose I deserved that.

The Captain pulled two maps from a satchel by his side, both wrapped in plastic.

"This is the world we left. Won't be needing it anymore." He tucked the larger map away and handed me the other.

"This is the one we're in now. See? Even the continents are different."

The other Goners clustered around me. Everything on the new map was warped out of shape.

"We're heading for Africa. All the continents began to fuse together near the end of the Jurassic period and it's the closest coastline east of New Hebrides."

"And you're sure it's actually there?"

"It's there." The Captain gave a contemptuous snort. "In the old days we had aeroplanes, before they ran out of aviation fuel. They confirmed it."

"How far did they scout?"

"Beats me. None of the planes who went farther than West Africa were ever heard from again."

We chugged along in silence until we saw a dirty pall drifting over the horizon.

"There's no smoke without fire." The Captain turned the boat towards the black spiral.

"It's got to be land."

The amphibious carrier rolled out of the surf and onto a stony beach with a throaty roar. On a large, flat rock a fire was indeed burning and it was man made. Orderly piles of sun bleached wood were heaped nearby, obviously collected by human hands. At least, I hoped it was human hands, and not the paws of some hairy, man-hunting ape creature.

The crew leapt out, weapons at the ready, leaving a Naval to man the cannon. At the end of the beach was a steep cliff, perhaps thirty feet high, studded with dark holes. We could see ferns and a few coniferous trees on the top.

Apart from that there was no sign of life. I can't say we were too upset about that.

Our relief didn't last long.

A knotted rope snaked out of one of the caves and a figure began to climb down. As he approached, we could see it was a man with a bushy white streaked beard and long hair. His skin was deep brown from years of exposure to the sun and he wore a loincloth of some kind of green leather. A bow and quiver of arrows were fastened across his knobbly back.

The soldiers levelled their guns at the stranger but the Captain signalled to hold their fire.

"My name is Davy Captain Jones," he called out. "My men and I mean you no harm."

The stranger ignored them, staring in naked fascination at our craft. Finally, he turned to the Captain.

"You're not Goners, are you?"

"*We* are." I waved my hand at the teenagers clustered behind me. I figured that admission would put me in the stranger's good graces and I was right. To the Captain's obvious displeasure, the stranger walked right past him and shook my hand.

"James Lookout Watt," he announced, nodding his head at the Soldiers and Scientists. "Who are those clowns?"

Davy Jones looked like he was about to explode.

"They want to do a deal with you," I replied, thinking on the spot. "They're searching for essential minerals to take back to New Hebrides. If you help them, they'll provide you with medical supplies and weapons when they leave."

"Is this true?" Watt addressed the Captain for the first time.

"It is." Davy Jones looked taken aback by how I'd handled the encounter. I kind of surprised myself, to be honest. Then again, I was Alan Carver, a born leader and genius to boot.

I was starting to quite enjoy my newfound confidence.

"Are there any more of you?" The Captain asked.

"A small colony living in cliff caves farther down the beach," James Watt replied. "I keep the fire burning as a beacon for new arrivals."

He turned back to the amphibious carrier.

"Never seen anything like *this* before."

"There were five of them when we set out," Jones said matter-of-factly. "The others didn't make it."

"It's not any safer here," Watt grunted. "I can't say you're welcome but we sorely need supplies. We always do."

"If your people will help, you can have everything in the boat when we leave."

"Then I'll take you to the others." Watt grinned, revealing a mouthful of rotten teeth. "If you'll give me a candy bar and a lift in that fine machine."

Watt told us the story of his colony as we rattled along the beach. He refused to engage with the representatives of New Hebrides but seemed happy to talk to fellow exiles. He had arrived here ten years ago, he told us, to a land which he called Pangea.

"Bet you're sorry you deserted now," one of the Soldiers sneered.

"Oh, I'm not a Goner," Watt replied pleasantly. "I was exiled for killing a man who angered me."

The Soldier lapsed into surly silence.

We listened in rapt fascination to the rest of the convict's tale, trying not to get too close to his stale breath.

Most Goners perished at sea, he explained, but enough made it to Pangea to start a small society. They lived in the cliffs because it kept them safe from predators, though they had to venture inland to hunt, an occupation fraught with danger. They avoided dinosaurs but small mammals were also present in this time period. That was their staple diet.

"Why do you stay here at all?" Florence asked. "Why not head east? Keep moving forward in time until you get to a place that's safer?"

"Some of the stronger ones attempted it," Watt sighed. "It's a perilous journey but they were determined."

"And?"

"Never made it." The man couldn't hide his bitterness. "You should go look for yourselves." He stared at the carrier floor. "A few more have tried over the years, with the same result."

He clasped his hands together miserably.

"We're trapped."

The carrier slewed to a halt below an even larger cliff. Wooden ladders rose from the beach to another set of caves and a cluster of ragged individuals peered down at us from their dark interiors. When we waved to them, they quickly retreated.

"We don't get many visitors," Watt explained. "Especially not armed to the teeth."

Leaving a Naval to guard the boat we followed the spindly figure up a ladder and into the first cave.

"I got a handful of new Goners," he called to the figures lurking in the darkness. "And some of

New Hebrides' finest, who'll give us supplies in exchange for our help."

A motley bunch of people emerged from the shadows, unkempt and wrapped in rudimentary outfits of fur or tanned leather. A couple still sported remnants of the uniforms they had worn on the island. They smiled shyly at us, ignoring the Captain and his men.

But one figure strode straight out of the darkness. His jacket was red and almost brand new. As I turned to greet him, he lashed out and punched me square in the mouth. I staggered backwards, hit the cave wall and fell flat on my back.

"Welcome to Pangea," The boy gave me a vicious kick in the ribs. "Remember me?"

I squinted up and groaned.

It was Elvis Regulator Presley.

<h1 style="text-align:center">-18-</h1>

The Pangean Council sat around the fire with the Captain and his men. Davy Jones had handed them all candy bars but, despite this, the air was heavy with suspicion. Elvis Presley had been included because he was the last Goner to reach Pangea alive and could attest to the sorry state of New Hebrides.

Now he was staring intently at me over the flames.

"I can't pretend this is anything but a business transaction," the Captain apologised. "I've seen how you live and I'm sorry, but I'm just following orders. Here's a list of the minerals we need."

The Council took his scrap of paper and handed it round.

"You can find most of these inland," the eldest said curtly. He was probably middle-aged but looked at least seventy. "I'll assign you a guide tomorrow, though I doubt anyone else will risk their lives to help New Hebrides' lackeys."

"Understood." Jones was equally straightforward. "If it's any consolation, I have grave doubts that we'll ever make it back. But we have to try."

The Scientists looked at him in alarm.

"What? You think the Megalodons will take a vacation for our return journey?"

"There are Plesiosaurs out there too," one Pangean broke in. "They're even bigger."

"Thanks."

"We have an empty cave your men can use to spend the night."

"We intend to sleep in our craft. We'll move it away from the cliffs in case your people decide to…"

He left the sentence unfinished but the implication was plain enough.

"Suit yourself. It won't end your problems."

"Explain."

"The amphibious carrier is big and grey. Looks like a carcass washed up on the beach." The Pangean leader shrugged. "It'll attract every night hunter within a ten-mile radius."

"Ok. I'm definitely staying in the caves." I stretched my arms out, enjoying the heat of the fire. "I can bunk down with you, Elvis."

I smiled winningly at him. My mouth was still sore from where he hit me.

"If you want," he replied, to my astonishment. "I'm still furious at you, but all Goners are welcome here. Hopefully, my snoring will keep you awake."

"I doubt I'll sleep much, anyway." Now that Jane Austen had found her colony, I was only too aware of her promise to kill me.

The Captain remained silent through our conversation.

"The new Goners can stay with you," he conceded eventually. "But my men and I will take our chances in the carrier. It's armoured, has a mounted gun and we'll post a watch. No offence."

"None taken." The Pangean leader picked at his rotten teeth. "We've made our dislike of you plain enough." He hesitated then indicated left. "Down the beach in that direction you'll find plenty of foliage. Cover the carrier with it. Dinosaurs are big, but they're stupid. That ought to fool them."

"I'm obliged."

"Pleasure is all mine," the Pangean grinned. "Wouldn't want some giant lizard munching its way through your pretty little boat."

"Then I'll bid you goodnight." Davy Jones stood up. "We'll collect the minerals and be out of your exceedingly long hair as soon as possible."

My group shared a small cave with Elvis Presley, who had been designated our official welcomer. And he certainly welcomed everyone but me, throwing his arms around the other kids and telling them of his fraught journey in a lone coracle to the shores of Pangea.

Despite his slim build, he was definitely one tough cookie.

Within a few minutes, most of my exhausted companions were asleep, protected by a fire burning in the cavern mouth. Elvis Presley and Jane Austen stayed awake, muttering together in a corner, flickering light from the flames moulding their shadowed faces into devilish masks.

I lay down with my head against the sharpest rock I could find. There was no way I was drifting off with those two plotting against me…

I woke up to find a sharpened flint pressed against my throat. Damn.

"That's to let you know I could kill you any time I wanted," Elvis whispered. "The only reason you're still alive is because I need help."

The other kids were bunched behind him, looking uncertain.

"This isn't the best start to our partnership," I swallowed hard. "I already have trust issues, what with being turned in by my own father and betrayed by my best friend."

Florence turned her face away.

"Get used to it," Elvis warned. "The Pangeans are about to do a number on you as well."

"I'm a Goner too," I protested. "I'm on their side now, remember?"

"Don't be too sure." Elvis removed the knife and sat back. "I've only been here a week but that's long enough to become very afraid of this crowd."

"They didn't exactly roll out the welcome mat." I sat up, rubbing my aching neck. "But I wasn't expecting Sea Tea and buns."

"You need a crash course on what life here is really like." Elvis tucked the flint back into his belt. "For a start, there *are* no minerals that can help you in this area. Despite what the Pangeans claim, there aren't many mammals either and the dinosaurs are too big or too fast to hunt. With that amphibious carrier, however, you could bring down any creature, no matter how large. Enough to give these people food for months."

He raised an eyebrow.

"They have no intention of letting it return to New Hebrides."

That came as no big surprise. Davy Jones thought so too, I imagined. Which is why he'd moved further down the beach.

"Then let's help them." I surprised myself by my own callousness. "We're trapped here as well. We don't owe the Captain anything."

The truth was, I was forming my own plan and I needed the carrier to make it work. I couldn't let it leave either.

"You don't understand." Elvis glanced cautiously around and lowered his voice. "The Pangeans have their own strict rules, same as New

Hebrides. Food is so scarce they're forced to take drastic measures."

I didn't like the sound of that.

"What kind of measures?"

"The current takes all Goners straight to this area, that's why we have a fire burning. The smoke can be spotted out at sea from miles away."

"What kind of measures, Elvis?"

"If we have enough to eat when a new Coracle arrives, the occupant is welcomed and that food is shared…"

"And if they *don't* have enough to eat?"

"That new arrival is their next meal." The boy shuddered.

"The Pangeans are cannibals."

I took a while to digest this information. Thinking on it, even the word digest made me a bit queasy.

"I don't want to be like the others, though I'm beginning to understand why they act this way." Elvis patted his stomach. "I've only been here a week and I'm absolutely starving."

"Winston Churchill is the fattest of us," I pointed out.

"Hold on now!" The boy backed away.

"I'm hungry but I'm not *that* hungry," Elvis responded quickly. "I want out of here before I get that way. That craft is my only hope of starting somewhere else and there's no way I can steal it myself."

He looked intently at me.

"That's where you come in."

"So." I took a deep breath. "All we have to do is get the ignition keys from the Captain, who is guarded by half a dozen heavily armed men. Then steal the amphibious carrier from under the noses of a colony of ravenous cannibals and assorted roaming dinosaurs. That about right?"

"If anyone can do it, it's Alan Carver."

Of course. He knew as well. That's why he hadn't pushed me off the rig.

"All right." I thought hard. "You need to make sure that you're picked as the guide tomorrow, Elvis. I'll wrangle a way to go too. From there we'll have to figure how to get control of the carrier and come back for the others. With that cannon on the craft, we should be able to call the shots."

"Nice plan." The boy smiled thinly. "But it's not going to work."

"And you know this… how?"

"The Pangeans lied to Captain Jones. Dinosaurs wouldn't dream of setting foot on the beach after dark." Elvis tiptoed to the cave entrance and made sure no eavesdroppers were lurking in the darkness. "Because every night swarms of Sea Lice emerge from the water looking for food."

"Sea Lice?"

"About the length of a finger with two deadly pincers on the front and an insatiable appetite. The foliage on the carrier will draw them like a magnet."

"So they eat leaves. What's the big deal?"

"They eat *everything*. They'll chew their way right through the canvas top on that craft to get at the people inside. In their thousands."

He winced at the thought.

"By morning there won't be anyone left alive on the beach."

<h1 style="text-align:center">-19-</h1>

"When do the Lice go back to the sea?" I asked.

"As dawn breaks. Then the Pangeans will stroll over and your vehicle will be empty for the taking."

"You got any weapons?"

"A bow and arrow. I've been practising with it night and day," Elvis replied dolefully. "Still haven't hit anything."

"Never mind." I pulled up my trouser legs to reveal a blaster tucked into each boot. "We need to get to that craft first."

The others stared at me.

"What?" I removed a gun and handed it to Elvis. "The Soldiers gave us access to their arms locker. None of you thought to swipe anything?"

"Of course." Florence lifted up her shirt, revealing a pistol.

"And me." Jane followed suit.

"I've got a weapon too." George Custer plunged a hand into his pants. "Of a different kind."

"Please don't."

"Chill." He gingerly withdrew a tube of Nitro-glycerine and placed it on a rock in front of him. "There ya go."

My eyes widened.

"You are a *very* brave kid, George Soldier Custer."

"So, got a new plan?"

As a matter of fact, I did.

"Elvis, do the Pangeans post guards or lookouts at night?"

"No point. The Sea Lice would get them and no other creatures venture onto the beach for the same reason."

"Jane. You take charge here." I jerked a thumb at the fire. "Build that up. Don't let anyone into this cave. Me and Elvis will climb the cliff and make our way along the top. Try to get as close to the carrier as we can before dawn."

"In the *dark*?" Florence glanced at her companions for backup. "That's insane!"

"Actually, it's possible." Elvis tapped his fingers together. "The main caves have fires in the entrances to keep flying pterosaurs away and they cast a glow up the cliff face. Enough to see hand and footholds, I bet."

"And light you up for the pterosaurs to spot." Jane joined in on Florence's side. "What if there are dinosaurs roaming the clifftops?"

I'd been trying not to think about that. But I couldn't come up with another course of action.

"There's a way around that, too." Elvis trotted to the back of the cave and came back with a battered plastic container. "Take a sniff of this."

He pulled off the lid and we all recoiled. The box was filled with dirty brown liquid. It stank like nothing I had ever encountered.

"Allosaurus pee," Elvis chuckled. "It's the biggest predator around and this is how it marks its territory. We collect it once the beast has gone."

"*There's* a job I wouldn't want." Winston Churchill wrinkled his nose.

"If we pour it over ourselves, no creature will come near us in case we turn out to be the real deal."

"Including me," Jane gagged.

"Come on then, tough guy." Elvis nudged the container towards me with his foot. "You first."

Reluctantly, I stripped down to my shorts. Florence blushed and Jane rolled her eyes. I tipped the foul liquid over my shoulders, letting it cascade down my body. Then I ran to the corner and threw up.

When I came back Elvis had done the same. Everyone else was standing several feet away holding their noses.

"Let's do this." I tucked the gun into my shorts.

"Ehm… John." Florence twiddled her thumbs. "What happens if you meet an actual Allosaurus?"

Oh, she just had to bring *that* up.

"We'll just have to hope it adopts us."

The glow from the fires below illuminated the cliffs, all right, but the light flickered and pulsed so that handholds vanished into shadow every few seconds. We made our way skywards at an agonisingly slow pace. My limbs ached after ten minutes and the fact that I stank like week old dead squid wasn't helping. The night was warm and muggy and soon I was covered in a sheen of sweat.

Elvis handled the climb better than I did. That didn't surprise me, recalling how he had shimmied up the rigs back on New Hebrides.

God, that seemed like a lifetime ago.

Inch by inch. Foot by foot, we finally made our way to the top. Elvis got there first, hauling himself over the fern covered rim. He swivelled round and held out his hand. I reached up, then hesitated.

"What?" he leered. "Afraid I'll let you fall this time?"

"The thought *had* occurred to me."

"Me too." He clasped my upstretched wrists. "I'm never going to like you, John, but you know how to fight. We're a team and that's that."

We made our way through shoulder-length ferns, blasters drawn, staying away from the trees that thickened into a solid block of shadows a few yards from the top. Gradually the ground began to slope down, indicating the cliffs were coming to an end.

"How will we know where the carrier is?" I whispered. "I doubt they're considerate enough to leave the headlights on."

As if on cue, we saw flashes a few hundred yards away, accompanied by the *putt putt* of automatic weapons.

"The Sea Lice have found them for us," the teenager replied blankly.

There was nothing we could do. We sat miserably in the dark listening to the gunfire peter out, to be replaced by screaming. I memorised the exact spot of the dying flashes and tried not to think of what was going on down there. Elvis clapped both hands over his ears.

When a crimson ring appeared along the horizon, he crawled over to me.

"The Sea Lice are retreating," he said. "Which means the Pangeans will be here any moment."

We jogged down the misty incline, trying not to trip over roots and rocks, then dropped onto the beach. As soon as we hit solid ground we sprinted.

All foliage covering the carrier had been stripped bare and there were skeletons scattered across the floor and on the beach, where some of the New Hebrideans had tried to make a run for it.

They never stood a chance. Even their clothes and hair had been devoured. All that was left of a group that had been living and breathing a few hours ago were bones, trinkets and rings.

Elvis tipped the skeletons in the vehicle onto the ground, with a shudder of disgust, while I checked the supplies. Fortunately, they were all in plastic containers and had survived the onslaught.

I finally found ignition keys under the seat. The Captain didn't even have a chance to start up the craft.

"You know how to drive this thing?" Elvis climbed into the turret.

"Looks pretty basic," I nodded. "Can you handle the big gun?"

"I'm a Regulator, same as you. Let's get moving and I'll work it out."

"No. We'll wait." I countered. "Have the Pangean's little war party come to us. Split their forces."

"You may be a horrible person," Elvis admitted grudgingly. "But you're a good tactician."

I supposed that was a compliment of sorts. I wasn't sure how to reply but tried to be nice back.

"I'm glad you weren't executed by the Town Council," I said lamely. "Really."

"Yeah. I'm sure it kept you awake at nights." Elvis ducked down from the gun turret. "Shhhh. Here they come."

We peered over the door. There were about ten warriors loping across the beach towards us, armed with homemade spears. A small party but I suppose nobody was expecting resistance.

Weren't *they* going to be in for a surprise?

I waited until the group was twenty yards away, before gunning the carrier into life.

Their faces were a picture. Surprise, then disbelief, then anger. A few of them launched spears as we roared past, but they bounced off the armoured sides of the carrier and we kept our heads down.

They immediately gave chase but our top speed was seventy miles an hour and, within seconds, we had left the group far behind.

As we approached the caves, I pulled over. Elvis looked at me quizzically.

"You drive," I said. "I'll man the cannon."

"Why?"

"Because you're a decent person and I'm not." It was beginning to dawn on me just how hard I could be. "You lived with this bunch, even if it was only for a week. You have a bond."

"You call them not *eating* me a bond?"

"I don't know. But I intend to get my people out, no matter what I have to do."

"*Your* people?"

"Yes. That includes you and anyone you want to bring."

"I haven't exactly made any friends," Elvis admitted, dropping into the driver's seat.

"Understandable. It'd be a bummer to wake up with your best bud munching your leg." I climbed into the gun turret and raised my hand.

"Let's roll."

I always wanted to say that.

-20-

There was a battle going on when we reached the cliffs. Jane Austen and Florence Nightingale were lying on the lip of her cave shooting down at the Pangeans, who were swarming up the steep face, homemade knives and slings clenched between their teeth. Winston, George and Napoleon rushed forwards threw a rock each and then retreated before the arrows being fired from the beach reached them.

"Looks like they noticed you and I were missing."

"Either that, or they're exceptionally peckish this morning."

The Pangeans gave a cheer when they saw the carrier, thinking it was manned by their own kind. A volley of automatic gunfire raking the cliff top and showering the climbers with debris soon set them right.

"Lay down your weapons," I shouted. "Or I'll turn you all into living colanders."

"Dead colanders," Elvis corrected.

"Yeah. Dead colanders!"

Reluctantly they climbed back to the beach and milled around in angry confusion. Jane threw down a rope ladder and led the others to ground level. Our party made their way apprehensively to the carrier and gratefully climbed in, while I covered them with the cannon.

"So that's it?" James Watt elbowed his way to the front of the Pangeans. "You're going to leave us here to starve?"

I stayed quiet. This was an argument I couldn't win.

"Look. We only want the carrier," he continued. "We can feed ourselves for years using its weapons. We've got no beef with you. Happy to have to join us, in fact."

The others in the craft looked at me uncertainly.

"I'll leave weapons, ammunition and supplies further down the beach," I replied firmly. "Even though you haven't honoured your side of the bargain."

"Where exactly do you think you're going to go?" Watt swept his arm around the beach. "This is all there *is*."

"We're going round the world."

The Pangeans stared in disbelief. Elvis and the others looked equally shocked.

"Say *what*?"

"There's no way you'll make it." Watt scoffed. "You're mere children."

"And your days are numbered," I retorted. "That's why there's no trace of you in the future."

Florence blanched.

"You could be a little more tactful," she hissed.

"Back west the whole human race is facing extinction." I stuck to my guns. "We need this carrier to save it. I'm sorry."

"So are we."

Watt gave a jerk of his head and his warriors surged forwards.

Elvis rammed his foot on the accelerator as they surrounded the craft. I swung the mounted cannon down before remembering it didn't point low enough to shoot anything below us. Instead, I jumped into the interior and began helping the others prise away the clutching fingers of men and women trying to scramble on board.

James Watt managed to climb inside and ran at me, knife raised. George Custer grabbed his arm and head-butted him in the face. With a swift kick, Jane dispatched him over the side.

Then we were free, roaring down the beach and sending up a spray of pebbles.

"What a rotten thing to do," Napoleon Bonaparte sobbed. "I feel sick."

"You want to go back and join them?" I snapped. "I'm quite prepared to let you."

"Of course not. But it doesn't make it any easier."

"We may have to do things a lot harder than this if we're going to live." Jane put her arm around the boy. "John Wayne made this decision so you wouldn't have to."

I felt a lump in my throat. She was the last person I expected to come to my defence.

"Sometimes being led by a ruthless psychopath has its advantages," she added acerbically.

Thanks for that, Jane.

We stopped a mile further on and Elvis and I took a quick dip in the ocean to wash away the stench of Allosaurus. Very quick - nobody had forgotten the Sea Lice. We picked out the best weapons and supplies for ourselves and left the rest on the beach for the Pangeans. The others wanted to leave a drum of fuel, but we had to keep the carrier moving as long as possible, so I forbade it. They muttered amongst themselves but eventually gave in.

I was beginning to realize how much being a leader sucked.

When the cliffs ended, we splashed into an inlet and headed east up a wide river. Once or twice we spotted huge alligator type things, but they weren't in the same class as the Megalodon and a couple of blasts from our cannon sent them sailing away.

When night began to fall we rolled ashore, found a clearing and built a fire.

I sat on my own, staring into the flames, while the others talked in low voices. I wasn't too worried about being killed in my sleep anymore but I had never felt so lonely.

Florence Nightingale came over and plonked herself beside me.

"You really think you can stop the human race from becoming extinct?"

"No," I admitted miserably. "I'm going to try, anyway."

"I've got your back." She slipped a hand into mine. "We all do."

"They hate me. Especially Jane."

"They'll come round. Even her. You're Alan Carver."

"I don't feel like much of a saviour."

"You don't look like one, neither," she smiled. "But you proved your worth today."

"Nobody make any sudden moves." George Custer slowly reached for a rifle and pulled it onto his lap. "We're being watched."

He nodded to his right. A dozen pairs of glittering eyes peered from the gaps between the trees at the edge of the clearing.

"What are the chances of those things being cute and cuddly?" Elvis slid his weapon out of its holster. "A million to one?"

"I like your optimism."

We were only ten yards from the carrier but we had no idea how fast the unidentified creatures could run, and we'd have to turn our backs on them to reach safety.

"When I give the signal, all of you fire in the direction of those beady little eyes. Then head for the vehicle and don't look round till you're aboard."

My companions pulled themselves into crouches, tense as wire.

"Now!" I shouted, pulling out my blaster and firing it over my shoulder. Then I was on my feet, dragging Florence with me.

The rest poured a volley into the trees, turned and ran.

Big mistake.

The Pangeans had known the power of our weapons and that was enough to stop them. To the creatures in the trees, gunfire was just a series of loud noises, and it sparked them into action.

I risked a glimpse back as I headed for sanctuary.

Our pursuers were man-sized, two-legged lizards with purple frills on their necks and long toothy snouts. They ran with a lolloping gait, holding nasty clawed forearms in front for balance.

And they were fast. Especially the leader, who had outstripped his companions and covered half the clearing already.

I reached the carrier and flung myself over the rim, scooping up a rifle from the floor.

Florence landed next to me, then Winston and Elvis. I leapt to my feet as Jane vaulted over the side and bounced off the driver's seat, followed by George Custer, still firing as he soared through the air.

The kid *was* good with weapons.

Napoleon Bonaparte was too short to jump that high. He was still trying to climb the side of the carrier when the dinosaur reached him. Jane grabbed his head to pull him in but the lizard snapped pointed teeth shut on his rucksack and yanked the boy into the air.

I raised my weapon but couldn't risk a shot. Napoleon was dangling from the jaws, face frozen in terror, obscuring most of the dinosaur. It began to retreat, carrying the screaming boy with it, trying to get its stubby arms up high enough to rip him open from behind. He kicked frantically at the talons, a hopeless effort to stay in one piece.

I don't know what came over me. Maybe it was because I'd left one group of people to their fate already. Maybe I was heartily sick of being at the mercy of fate.

Maybe I just wanted my companions to respect me.

I dived from the carrier, twisting in mid-air, and landed on the reptile's back. As it bucked and writhed, trying to dislodge me, I pushed the rifle under its forelegs and pulled back, trapping the talons against its body.

The creature released Napoleon and began to twirl around, like a dog chasing its tail, desperate to get those pointy teeth into my flesh. The other lizards circled, ready to pounce, while my companions tried to get a bead on the frantic animal without hitting me.

"Stay down!" I yelled at Napoleon. Then I pulled the trigger.

The rifle was set on automatic. As the monster pranced around, roaring in frustration, a stream of bullets sprayed in all directions. Three of the dinosaurs keeled over, spouting blood and the rest retreated, realising we weren't defenceless as they'd thought.

The creature suddenly sank down and rolled over, trying to trap me under its bulk. I flung myself backwards, landing on my bum. The dinosaur reared over me and opened its jaws.

"Aaaaaaaaaargh!" Napoleon Bonaparte shot past and slammed a Pangean spear into the beast's neck. It gave a surprised cough and toppled over, spasming violently, blood mingling with the trampled ferns.

Napoleon pulled me to my feet and we clambered into the carrier. Elvis pointed the cannon at the tree line, where the rest of the attackers were cowering and opened fire.

Leaves, trunks and dinosaurs dissolved in a torrent of lead. When he finally stopped, the edge of the forest and everything in it had been torn apart.

The others surrounded me, clapping my back and talking all at once. Napoleon shook my hand vigorously and Florence kissed me on the cheek.

"Told you," she winked.

Jane Austen stood back, hands on her hips. When the furore had died down, she came over and poked me in the chest.

"That was very stupid. And… quite noble."

"Your smart comment to follow?"

"Perhaps I won't kill you yet. It's too much fun watching you get knocked around."

"I appreciate it."

"I'll take first watch." She climbed into the gun mounting and patted Elvis on the shoulder. "Nice shooting, by the way."

"Not really." The boy shrugged. "I was aiming at John."

I lay down on the floor of the carrier, Florence next to me, pressed against my back for warmth.

"Goodnight, Alan Carver," Napoleon called. "Thanks for rescuing me."

"Thanks for covering my back."

"You got it, boss."

I'd been up for almost two days straight but I still found it hard to get to sleep. It wasn't the threat of another attack that kept me awake.

I just couldn't stop grinning.

-21-

We wouldn't have survived one day without the carrier. Its armoured hull protected us from predators when we were afloat and the reinforced wheels could handle most terrains. We slept in the vehicle at night and used it to chase down food.

Even so, the journey east was fraught with danger. We soon learned to avoid forests. The trees slowed us down to a crawling pace and, now that the canvas top was chewed away, its denizens had the nasty habit of dropping out of overhanging branches into the open cab.

Honestly. This thing was made of inch-thick armour plating but nobody thought to put on a metal *roof*?

When we could, we used the rivers, much faster and less dangerous than travelling through woodland. We rejoiced when we came across a flat plain because the vehicle could drive at top speed and the noise of its diesel engines scared away all but the largest carnivores. When they attacked we used the cannon.

That was a Godsend too. Sometimes there was no way to proceed but through the forest, so we used it to blast away fallen trees and thick root systems. The downside was, after three days, we were running dangerously low on shells. Our group still had plenty of small arms but I knew they couldn't bring down carnivores like Spinosaurus or Gigantosaurus.

I'd learned the names from Florence and Jane, who had read all of Robert Lee's books and now possessed an enviable knowledge of Earth's history. Jane had finally stopped giving me the cold shoulder and, though I didn't completely trust her, there was no doubt the girl's expertise saved us more than once.

"You may not rate books," she said sagely. "But thanks to reading, I know my enemy."

I wasn't sure if I was still included in that category.

Our biggest problem was the Pterosaurs. It turned out the gun mounting didn't point straight upwards either, so we had to use concentrated small arms fire to scare them away. That took its toll on our ammo too. More than once, I wished I could get my hands on the stupid scientists who designed the carrier. No wonder they never found a bloody cure for the Golden Plague.

On the morning of day four we were still alive and facing a plain that stretched to the horizon. Giant herds of Ankylosaurs grazed on the short spiky grass, creating a haze of emerald fog. With a whoop, Winston Churchill revved our vehicle to top speed, weaving through the startled animals.

"Shouldn't we be approaching some sort of time rift soon?" Napoleon Bonaparte was lying on a tipped back seat, partly to relax, partly to keep an eye on the skies for Pterodactyls. "According to the colony we left behind, it was like a conduit that moved their explorers into the future."

To be honest, I was in awe of any Pangeans who had tried to make it this far. How tough were *they*? Maybe we should have invited a couple along.

"I don't get it." Napoleon persisted. "If there are time portals *we* can get through, why can't anything else? Why can't the dinosaurs?"

"Got no idea whatsoever."

"But you're Alan Carver."

"The original Alan Carver was a famous scientist," I pointed out. "I'm a Regulator, in case you hadn't noticed. They're somewhat different fields."

"Yeah, but you're still a genius."

Jane Austen coughed derisively into her hand.

"All right." I was determined not to give her the satisfaction of looking stumped. "The Sixth Ring messed everything up. As far as I can see, it didn't just move New Hebrides forwards through the years, it displaced it in time entirely."

"Go on."

"So anything that originated in New Hebrides can breach the barriers between the time periods because it doesn't really belong anywhere."

"I know *that* feeling," Florence said sadly.

"We belong to each other," Winston said brightly. "We're Goners."

"Yeah," Napoleon agreed. "We're a gang now."

"You two have certainly come out of your shells," I grunted. "Right into the realm of miserableness. Goners isn't a badge of honour. It's a criticism."

"Got a better name?"

"The Techno-Annihilation Squad?" I suggested hopefully. "It has a certain ring."

"Who votes to keep calling ourselves Goners?" Jane stuck up her hand. "John Wayne obviously hates the idea."

Every hand shot up and Florence laughed out loud.

Great. They were *proud* to be convicts.

An hour later George Custer, who had taken over driving, slewed to a halt.

"That what I think it is?"

There was a shimmering, sparkling haze in front of us, stretching from North to South as far as the eye could see. A herd of Ankylosaurs passed right through it, then out the other side, without even noticing. I didn't think the same thing would happen to us if we ventured into that glittering curtain.

"How much fuel do we have?"

"Half a tank and four drums in the back."

"That seems an awful lot."

"It does, doesn't it?" Elvis looked at the odometer and did a quick calculation. "Wow. We could travel a few thousand miles with that."

A little warning bell went off in my head. Why so much fuel? And why had the Town Council put so few people in each carrier?

Then again, I was a Regulator and we're suspicious by nature. I pushed it to the back of my mind.

"We also have half a drum of Allosaurus Pee that Winston collected from a puddle a couple of days ago."

"Knew I'd get that job," the boy mumped.

"Pour it over the carrier. According to Jane, dinosaurs got even bigger as time passed. It might help keep them away."

"Glad to be rid of it." Elvis hefted the container onto his shoulder and began to splash the contents over the hood. "If anyone wants to dab it behind their ears for extra protection, I won't be sitting near them."

"Water?"

"We got plenty." George held up a brace of canteens.

"Ammo?"

"The cannon is almost out." Florence ticked off statistics on her fingers. "The blaster batteries are a quarter used. Our automatic rifles have about a hundred rounds each. Oh. We also have one bow, seven arrows and a couple of knives."

"Will they pass through the barrier?" Winston asked. "They're from here, not New Hebrides."

"I heard one of the Scientists say he had a theory that we make a hole when we go through," Napoleon replied. "Anything right next to us comes along for the ride."

"Let's make sure it's not an Allosaurus." Florence looked around anxiously. "Nope. All clear."

"Let's not bother about the old-school weapons, huh?" George snorted. "They're a last resort."

Hah. That was only because he didn't know how to use them.

"Our fists are the last resort." I stood up and squinted through the windscreen. Just remember, a bunch of Pangeans with spears tried to reach this barrier. I think I ran over their bones about half a mile back."

"That's encouraging."

"They weren't Goners." I gave the others my most determined look. "Hands up who's ready for this?"

Nobody moved.

"Excellent." I raised my arm above my head and swept it forward. "Onward troops!"

George sighed and moved off again.

For a second we were surrounded by sparks and then the landscape warped around us, folding in upon itself until we were spat out on the other side.

And found ourselves in hell.

-22-

The grassy plain had turned into a dusty, ochre desert and the heat was almost unbearable. Far off to the north, a volcano spewed sulphurous clouds into a glowering orange sky.

"Look behind you." Elvis turned my head around.

The barrier was gone and desert stretched away as far as I could see.

"That's why nobody ever came back," he said unhappily. "It's a one-way ticket."

"Looks like it," I agreed. "This place is about as hospitable as Jane."

"Jane can hear," the girl grunted. "You big lout."

"Full speed ahead, George." Elvis wiped his forehead with a grimy sleeve. "We need to get to the next time period before we fry."

The landscape we travelled through was as un-changing as it was unforgiving. And there was no sign of life.

"You're the history experts," I turned to Jane and Florence. "Where do you think we are?"

"It seems likely this is the end of the Cretaceous Period." Florence's hair was already sticking to her brow. "Massive volcanic eruptions and climate change caused the dinosaurs to start dying out."

"That's one less thing to worry about."

"They're not gone yet. Most were killed by a giant meteor hitting the earth."

"Can't this thing go any faster? I glanced up anxiously.

"The Cretaceous period lasted about 54 million years." Florence gave a wry smile. "We'd have to be pretty unfortunate to arrive just as a comet was going to hit."

"How's our luck been so far?"

"I hear you." She tapped George on the shoulder. "Can't this thing go any faster?"

"We're overheating as it is." The boy had wrapped a scarf around his face. "Which is making the Allosaurus smell wafting off the bonnet a real pain in the bum, by the way."

And so we drove. A hundred miles. Then three hundred. Then seven hundred. Nothing changed.

"Explain it to me again." Napoleon and Winston were sheltering in the rear of the carrier, with fern leaves over their heads to fend off heatstroke. "If we travel right round the world, always moving forward in time, we'll eventually end up back where we started?"

"That's right." Winston held the Captain's map, still wrapped in plastic, on his knee. "In this era, Pangea becomes one giant land mass, which is why we can cross from West Africa to Asia without hitting water. But it *will* eventually split into different continents again. If we still have enough fuel to cross the water, we'll end up on the east coast of North America in the 21st century, just as the Golden Plague is taking over the earth."

"Suppose we find out who started the Plague while we're on the way. Couldn't we stop them?"

"If we prevent it happening," Winston sighed. "New Hebrides won't become the last refuge of the human race. The Sixth Ring will never be used. None of us will ever be born. So we won't be *able* to go back in time."

"But we *have*."

"Exactly. Which means none of us managed to stop the wheat. We might have tried but we obviously failed."

"How can we have already *failed*?" Napoleon clutched his head. "It's in the future."

"The future for this time period, yes," Winston said patiently. "But it doesn't stop it being in New Hebrides' past."

"Aw, just give up Winston." Jane Austen was lying across the rear of the carrier soaking up the sun. "There are dinosaurs who'll get the concept before Napoleon does."

"No, no. Hear me out." The boy shut his eyes and concentrated. "Ok. Ok. Suppose we reach the east Coast of America in the 21st century. What if we keep going? Wouldn't we travel forward even further and end up back on New Hebrides over a century later? Right about when we left, in fact."

"I don't *know*."

"I certainly hope so," Jane yawned. "Then you can try and explain it to yourself. See how frustrating *that* is."

"I could meet myself?" Napoleon's eyes widened. "How cool would that be? If we had a fight, which one of us do you think would win?"

"That's not going to happen," Winston slapped his companion with the map. "You never met yourself when you were on the island, did you? If you had, don't you think you'd *remember* it?"

"Hell yeah. First thing I'd do would be talk myself out of deserting."

"Yet, here you are bugging me."

"Stop talking, Winston," I warned. "You're making my brain sore."

Napoleon tapped his fingers doubtfully against his lip.

"Explain it to me again…"

After four days, there was still no sign of life. Our food stocks were running low and so was the water. We took turns at driving while the others napped under seats, trying to shield ourselves from the punishing glare of the sun. Sometimes we stood in the gun turret letting the breeze cool our faces. Our skin went red, then bronze as we adjusted to the climate.

"You're going to end up the same colour as me," Winston laughed.

On the fourth day, Florence came and sat beside me. Her skin was nut brown and she had cut her hair short with a knife to stop it being permanently plastered to her face. She was used to scant rations and had actually filled out. She looked nothing like the pale, fragile teenager she had been on New Hebrides.

"You seem pretty worried," she said.

"I am. Who knows how far we are from the next time shift? The Pangeans can't have made it anything like this far. "

"Probably not. But we've left the volcanoes far behind and the sky looks less angry. Temperature's dropping too."

She was right. A day later, flowers began to appear on the boulder strewn prairie and we finally spotted animals, a herd of Triceratops grazing in the distance. A few hours later, we reached a huge lake, ringed by fir trees and giant thistles.

"Check *that* out," Elvis breathed.

In the middle of the vast expanse of water, a family of Brontosaurus were dipping their snakelike necks under the surface and emerging with trailing weeds grasped in their peg-like teeth. They paid us no attention, too large and far out to be worried by any intruder, even one that smelled of Allosaurus pee.

We parked and stumbled down to the water, filling our canteens and splashing the cool liquid on our faces. Once we were satisfied no aquatic monster was lurking in the shallows, we decided it was safe to swim.

"Me and Florence will go first," Jane announced. "And we'll be naked, so keep that carrier nice and far away."

"But we have to cover you," Elvis objected.

"Fair enough, but no peeking until we're in the water." Jane put her hands on her hips, a sure sign that she meant business. "I'll yell if something starts eating Florence."

"In that case, we're going hunting." Napoleon and Winston grabbed a rifle each. "We saw some little lizardy things hiding in the trees."

"Don't get too far away," I said quickly. "And be very careful."

"What are you? Our dad?"

"Would your dad shoot you for disobeying orders?"

"You got it, boss," they saluted.

"Kids," I tutted. "They grow up so fast."

As soon as they were gone Elvis, George and I clambered into the gun turret, elbowing each other to get the best view. The girls were up to their necks, but whenever they swam we got a tantalising glimpse of flesh.

"Jane is *so* cute." Elvis leaned a hand on his chin. "Wish I had the nerve to tell her, but I think she has a sneaky liking for you, John."

"Why? Cause she hasn't killed me in my sleep?"

"It's Florence who's seriously hot," George argued. "I'm nuts for a girl with brains as well as guns. Which one do you like, John?"

They turned to me. In the cramped confines of the turret, their noses were pressed against my face.

"Personal space, lads."

"This is all the room there is. Don't avoid the question."

"Actually, I quite fancy them both."

I hadn't even realised the fact until the words were out of my mouth. Well… maybe I had, but I didn't want to admit it. Turning crimson was not a good quality in a leader.

"Coming out now," Jane shouted. "Avert your eyes, boys. Don't make us come up there and kill you."

We climbed down and turned our backs until the ladies got dressed. Then it was our turn.

The water was wonderful. We splashed each other, swam and then just lay on our backs and floated.

"You think the girls are watching?" Elvis asked self-consciously.

"It's a fair bet." George spat a fountain of water into the air. "They're both in the gun turret with a pair of binoculars."

"We have *binoculars*?"

"Yeah, I forgot to tell you."

Once we were dressed, we sat around the carrier letting the sun dry our hair. All of us were quiet and a little embarrassed.

"What's taking the time-travel twins so long?" I stood up and looked anxiously around. "Maybe we should go look for them."

"There they are." Elvis pointed. "Look pretty excited too. They must have caught something."

Winston and Napoleon raced towards us, waving their arms.

"What are they saying?" I waved back. "I can't hear."

"Start a fire?" Elvis cupped his ear. "Nope. Something about… bending?"

George was suddenly on his feet and clambering into the cab.

"They're shouting *start the engine*."

An earth shattering shriek split the stillness. The Brontosaur's heads shot up and they retreated further into the lake, submerging their great shiny bodies.

The pine trees shook and parted and the most terrifying thing I had ever seen burst into the clearing. It had to be forty feet from tip to tail. Its head alone was half the length of the carrier.

And those teeth. My God, the *size* of those teeth.

"Go! Get the hell out of here!" Florence gasped, helping Winston and Napoleon on board.

"That's a Tyrannosaurus Rex."

-23-

George didn't need a second telling. The carrier roared towards the water, wheels spinning in the dirt and churning up flowers.

"Not the lake!" Elvis yanked at the wheel. "It's got a sandy shore. We'll get stuck before we're far enough out to float."

George veered back onto the prairie, the T-Rex in hot pursuit.

I couldn't believe something so big could move at that speed. It was actually *gaining* on us, viscous strings of drool trailing from its open mouth.

"Speed it up, George!" I slapped the back of his neck. "You're only doing forty miles an hour."

"Big rocks everywhere!" The boy jerked the wheel to the left and I was slammed against the door. "We hit one and it'll tear the axle right off."

"Do your best." I scrambled into the turret and swung the cannon to point out the rear of the craft. But it would only go halfway round.

"What were the people who built this bloody thing *thinking*?" I roared. "About what they wanted for lunch?"

"It's what the T-Rex is thinking, for sure. And that would be us." Florence squinted down the barrel of her gun and poured a volley into the beast. It didn't even flinch. "Our small arms are having no effect, by the way."

"Aim for its eyes."

"We're bouncing up and down so much, I can't even *see* its eyes."

I spotted another herd of Triceratops in the distance.

"Head over there!"

George spun the wheel again.

We reached the trundling herbivores with the Tyrannosaurus only twenty feet behind. Most of the creatures broke into a run, but the biggest males stood their ground, shoulder to shoulder, presenting us with a wall of horns.

I raked the ground in front of the beasts and they shuffled away from the ricocheting bullets, surprised rather than hurt. George rammed his foot on the gas and shot through the gap before they had a chance to close ranks.

The T-Rex knew it would be impaled if it tried the same route. Instead, it skirted the defences, roaring in fury, still fixated on us.

Because of their armour and horns, the Triceratops didn't need to be particularly fast. Within seconds we had caught up with the rest of the fleeing herd. Fortunately, the creatures couldn't use their main defence against us while they were running.

"They got the same design flaw as the carrier," Elvis chuckled. "No wonder they became extinct."

He just *had* to say that.

The herd shuddered to a grinding halt, snorting clouds of vapour into the air. Then they slowly turned and faced us.

"Back up, George! Back up!"

"He can't." Winston moaned. "The big males have turned and are coming up behind."

One beast abruptly charged, ramming his three-pronged horns into the carrier's side. The vehicle was almost toppled over and an ivory point came right through the door, narrowly missing Florence's arm.

I opened fire again. I hadn't wanted to use any more cannon shells but these monsters were more dangerous than the T-Rex. The beasts in front of us retreated in panic, flowers of red blossoming on their thick hides. The carrier moved into the gap.

Another attacked from the rear, bucking the back of the vehicle.

"Why are they acting like this?" Napoleon wailed. "They're plant eaters."

"We're covered in Allosaurus pee." Elvis threw away his exhausted blaster and picked up another. "They think *we're* a predator."

"Go diagonally, George." I swung the big gun and began blasting a path through the stamping, snorting creatures. "We've got to get out the other side of this herd."

"Go forward. Go back. Go diagonally." The boy spun the wheel again. "Isn't a leader supposed to be decisive?"

"Fine. Head straight back toward the T-Rex, if you want. It's still there."

"I'll go diagonally."

The largest Triceratops were longer than the carrier and must have weighed over five tons. Their hides were plated and covered in rivet-like lumps of gristle. Small arms fire did no more than frighten them and, though the cannon could dent their armour, it wasn't coming close to bringing one down. We ran a deadly gauntlet between the enormous bodies, weaving and firing.

"I take back what I said about their design flaw," Elvis muttered.

But the sheer surprise of encountering an adversary who could harm them had the desired effect. The creatures in front of the carrier retreated, opening a space we could drive through.

"We're almost there," Jane cried, as two giant, dusty butts parted to show us the plain stretching ahead.

Her jubilation came too soon. As we emerged from the herd, one Triceratops made a final enraged thrust, head lowered. Its horns smashed into the carrier just above the front wheels, ripping through the chassis and shattering the windscreen.

But we were out, speeding across the prairie, black smoke pouring from under the wheel rim.

The Triceratops bunched back into formation and carried on their way as if we had never been there. Made me feel a little insignificant, to be honest. I spotted the T Rex on the other side of the herd, still watching us but unable to get past the trundling leviathans. It still looked *plenty* interested.

We limped east until it was out of sight, but I was sure we hadn't seen the last of our pursuer.

"That was a close one, eh Winston?" Jane elbowed the boy but he slumped back in his seat, eyes closed.

"Winston?"

"Oh my God," Florence knelt beside him. "Look at his leg."

I climbed down from the turret, heart sinking. There was a deep, bloody gash running from Winston's knee, all the way to the top of his thigh.

"Get a medical kit," Elvis shouted. "We have to stop and fix this."

"Not till we're farther away from that Tyrannosaurus." I leaned out of the carrier and inspected the wheels. A lump of misshapen metal was sticking out of the chassis, which I imagined was probably vital to the vehicle working properly. "This thing might break down any minute."

"It's just a dumb beast." Elvis ripped open Winston's trouser leg and began cleaning away the blood while Florence inspected the wound. "It will have forgotten us, just like the Triceratops."

"It's a territorial animal," Jane corrected. "It won't quit till it finds us."

"This one, especially." Napoleon was hunched miserably in the corner. "Me and Winston just shot its young."

"You *what*?"

"We thought they were just little dinosaurs." The boy began to cry. "We didn't know they were Tyrannosaur babies."

"The wound needs stitches, *now*." Florence was close to tears as well. "I can't stop the bleeding."

"Then stitch it," I rasped. "We've got surgical thread and needles in the medical kit."

"I *can't* while the carrier is bumping around."

"You have to stop, John," Elvis insisted. "We can hold the T-Rex off with our cannon."

"I used up all the shells on the Triceratops." I slammed my hand against the gun mounting in frustration. "We've no way to defend ourselves."

"George still has a tube of Nitro-glycerine," Elvis persisted.

"We can only use that if the T-Rex is right on top of us. That's too close for my liking."

"Let me off. I'll take that chance."

I hated myself for what I said next.

"I'm not swapping the life of a trained Regulator for a boy who can't even walk."

"He'll *die* if we don't do something," Florence sobbed. "Alan Carver would never allow that."

"Do I stop or not?" George glanced anxiously back.

I ran a hand down my face, close to panic. If the T-Rex had given up, I'd be letting Winston die for nothing. But what if it hadn't? Out here, with no cannon, we wouldn't stand a chance.

What *would* Alan Carver do?

"Keep going," I commanded. "You'll have to bind his leg with bandages."

Elvis stood up and placed his blaster against my head.

"Stop the damned vehicle."

Florence lashed out with one hand and the gun dropped to the ground.

Elvis staggered back, clutching his wrist.

"John's our leader," she snarled. "We obey, whether we agree with him or not."

George swerved to avoid a large red mound of earth and Jane's eyes widened.

"Wait. Can we stop for one minute?" She grabbed my arm. "Just *one*."

"That's not long enough to stitch up..." I began.

"Trust me!"

Those were words I never expected to come out of Jane Austen's mouth.

"All right, but I'll be counting. Pull over, George."

Before the carrier had stopped moving, Jane grabbed the medical kit, emptied it out and jumped over the side, heading towards the mound. She knelt and scraped the plastic container along the ground, then sprinted back, slapping at her legs.

As soon as she was in the cab, I signalled for George to carry on. We crowded round the girl in puzzlement.

"Fire ants." She opened the kit to reveal inch-long red insects scurrying around the interior. "Look at the pincers on those things."

"You better have a good reason for this." Elvis was still holding his wrist. "Your friend is bleeding to death."

"Hold Winston's wound shut."

Five pairs of hands did so. Mercifully, the boy had lapsed into unconsciousness.

Jane picked up an insect and held it against his injured leg. The ant clamped curved mandibles shut on either side of the gash, closing that section. She twisted the body off, leaving its head locked in place.

"These things never let go," she explained. "Not even when they're dead."

"That is genius." Elvis stared at her. "I totally forgive you."

Jane turned to me, fists balled.

"I don't forgive *you*, though. You just got lucky, is all."

We drove as fast as we dared for the next hour, Florence holding a damp cloth to Winston's head. The engine was beginning to make a knocking noise I really didn't like.

"Steering's getting sluggish." George confirmed my fears. "I think these beasties did some real damage."

"All right." I finally gave in. "Soon as we find shelter, we'll stop and have a proper look. See if we can repair it."

The carrier suddenly halted.

"Would that count as shelter?" George said quietly.

We looked in the direction he was pointing.

"Now, *there's* something you don't see every day."

The object in front of us was derelict, rusted and overgrown with creeping tendrils.

"What *is* it?" I asked.

"That?" Jane's voice was filled with awe.

"It's an aeroplane."

-24-

We climbed out of the vehicle and cautiously approached.

"It's one of the exploration planes from New Hebrides," Napoleon said. "Has to be."

"Where do you think the pilot is?"

"Forget it. He's long dead." Elvis pulled a strand of dry ivy from the cracked hull. "This thing's been here for over a century."

I decided this was as good a time as any to re-assert my authority.

"George. Take a weapon and check there's nothing dangerous inside. Elvis and Florence? Get Winston out of the sun. We can put him in the plane once George gives the all-clear."

"I'll check the interior too." Jane unshouldered her rifle. "See if there's anything useful we can salvage."

"Napoleon? Get under the vehicle and see how bad the damage is."

"Will do. Give me a shout if that T-Rex appears."

"Maybe," I said, light-heartedly. "Then again, we might need you to act as a decoy."

Nobody laughed. All our camaraderie had drained away after that last encounter. Despite our banter and tough talk, it brought home the fact that we were a bunch of teenagers, lost in a deadly alien landscape with a leader who didn't really know what he was doing.

That would be me.

"Nothing deadly in here," George shouted. "Unless you count yours truly."

I hunched down by the carrier as the others carried Winston inside.

"What's the story, Napoleon?"

"Good job we stopped when we did." The Mechanic popped his head out. "The side panel is buckled out of shape and pressing against the front wheels. Hasn't done too much damage, but we need to straighten it out or the friction will eventually shred the tyres and crack the axle."

"What do you need?"

"A big hammer to pound out the dents or some kind of metal cutter to sheer off the side entirely."

"Could I shoot it away?"

"Not unless you want the ricochet to take your head off."

We sat in the mossy interior of the plane while Napoleon explained our predicament. Florence was outside, standing guard.

"It's pretty empty inside," Jane reported sadly. "But I found a weapon."

She handed me a wooden catapult, just like the one I used to play with when I was a little boy.

"It was wrapped in an oily rag and hidden under the dashboard."

"Calling this a weapon is like saying the carrier has a paint scratch."

"It *is* a weapon. And it was important enough to the pilot to make sure it survived all this time."

"Can't imagine why."

I tested it. Despite its age, the elastic was still stretchy, probably because of the oil. It seemed a weird thing to protect and hide. I'd have thought any stranded pilot would have more pressing things to think about. Like not getting eaten.

"The plane itself isn't going to offer much protection," Jane continued. "It's nothing but a rusty shell held together by plant roots."

"Could things get any worse?" Napoleon put his head in his hands.

Florence scrambled up the wheel hatch.

"There's a dust cloud approaching." She swallowed hard. "No prizes for guessing what it is."

Out of the blue, I thought about Mum and Dad. Wondered if they remembered me fondly, now that they undoubtedly had a new baby son. Well, I'd make my parents proud, even if they'd never know it.

"Pass me the tube of Nitro-Glycerine, George." I tested the catapult again. "This might give us a fighting chance."

"It might. If you were fighting a six-year-old."

"The rest of you, cover me." I ignored the jibe. "Try to keep the T-Rex distracted so I can get close."

"No." Elvis placed a hand on my arm. "You were right and I was wrong. I'll go."

"I wasn't right." I seemed to be saying that a lot lately. "The plane isn't a better defensive position than our carrier. The T-Rex will rip apart this bucket of bolts in seconds."

"Ah, but I have an idea." Elvis wagged a finger at me.

"Getting torn limb from limb isn't any sort of plan."

"That was *your* plan," Florence added unhelpfully.

"All right," I said. "I'll give you the Nitro if you can convince me."

"Keep it." Elvis turned and jumped out of the hatch before I had time to stop him. "Time you saw a real Regulator at work."

He ran to the carrier, vaulted in and began gathering up the bloody bandages we'd used to wrap Winston's leg.

"What's that idiot doing?" I pocketed the tube of explosives and made to go after him. Jane grabbed me by the scruff of the neck.

"Give him a chance," she said. "He's trying to save face and say sorry."

"I'm not looking for an apology." I seethed. "Despite what you all might think, I don't want any of your deaths on my conscience."

"Good. I was beginning to think you didn't have one." Jane let go. "But I think I know what he's up to."

Elvis was wrapping the bloody bandages round the carrier's twisted side panel. The T-Rex appeared over the horizon and headed towards him.

Suddenly I got it.

"Hold your fire everyone," I instructed.

The Tyrannosaurus closed the distance at a run, puffs of dirt erupting with every one of its six ton steps. Elvis climbed down and waited calmly beside the vehicle. A hundred yards. Then fifty. Then twenty.

The T-Rex opened its slavering mouth in anticipation.

I could hardly bear to watch.

As it lunged to snap the teenager in two, Elvis crouched and slid under the vehicle. The jaws clamped on empty air and the T-Rex reared back in fury. Then it spotted the bandages covered in human blood.

With an enraged scream, it clamped its teeth on the broken panel and pulled with all its might.

"Now you can go." Jane slapped me on the back.

I dived out of the hatch. The Tyrannosaurus was shaking its head from side to side, stubby forelimbs clawing at the carrier, too preoccupied to notice me running towards it. With a screech of tortured metal, the entire side panel was wrenched from the vehicle and flung into the air, landing fifteen feet away.

One eye rolled round, looking for its next victim.

That would be me.

I was so close I could smell the heat wafting from its body. Too near to miss. I placed the tube of nitro in the catapult sling.

"Should have stuck to the prey you know best, big guy."

I pulled back the elastic and let go.

The tube hit the T-Rex's thick hide and exploded. I was thrown backwards by the force of the blast, landing against one of the rocks with an agonising jolt.

The monster tried to claw at the gaping hole where its chest used to be, but it no longer had any arms. With an agonised grunt, it fell over and lay still.

"You can come out from under the carrier now, Elvis," I said shakily, staggering to my feet. "You've… eh… fixed it."

The boy scrambled into view, goggling at the fallen giant.

"Can't believe that actually worked." He trotted over to me. "I think we did pretty well, all in all."

"Didn't catch that." I wiped blood from my nose. "My ears won't stop ringing."

I began to shake. I was *alive*. We were *all* alive.

Elvis caught me as my legs gave way.

I woke up on a bed of green moss in the cool interior of the plane, Florence holding my hand. Winston Churchill was awake, lying next to me.

"Welcome back, boss," he grinned. "Only room for one slacker on this expedition."

"What's that smell?" My mouth was watering.

"T-Rex." Jane thrust a chunk of steaming meat at me. "Only fair. It would have been happy enough to eat *us*."

I took a bite.

"Tastes like chicken."

"You've no idea what chicken tastes like." Elvis loomed over me.

"I want to apologise," he said sheepishly. "I should have known to believe Alan Carver."

"Alan Carver didn't save us." I took another bite. "Elvis Presley did."

"So did John Wayne." He crossed his heart theatrically. "I won't question you again."

"Question all you like. This isn't New Hebrides." I leaned back and closed my eyes. "But no more pointing guns at me, please."

Later I sat with Florence, watching the glow from the fire flickering through the hatch. Winston and Napoleon were asleep. George, Elvis and Jane were outside and we could hear them laughing and talking.

"You go join them," I said. "Honestly, I'm fine."

"I've faced death so many times in the last few days." Florence picked a strand of ivy from the fuselage and pushed it into her hair. "And yet…"

"You still have time to be fashionable?"

"How I feel about you scares me more than anything."

"What do you mean?" But I had already guessed the answer.

"We could be killed at any time." She took a deep breath. "Seems dumb to be afraid of saying how much I care about you."

"Florence. I'm a bully who never thinks of anyone but himself."

"Oh, you were. But not anymore."

"That's not necessarily a good thing." I reached out and took her hand. "I can't afford to get attached to one person when my job is to keep you *all* safe."

"You like Jane." Florence's mouth twitched. "I understand. She's strong and doesn't take any crap. Perfect partner, really."

I thought long and hard about that. I was attracted to Jane, no doubt about it, especially since she was no longer determined to murder me. But I'd always liked Florence and, now the grime of New Hebrides had washed off, I realised how pretty she was.

The old me surfaced for a moment. Maybe I could have them both. I was their leader, after all.

But Florence was right. I had changed. I wanted to be Alan Carver more than I wanted to be John Wayne, and I'd been given a chance to do just that.

"I care about you, too," I said. "More than you realise. I won't deny I like Jane, but my priority is getting this whole group to safety. It's what I have to concentrate on."

"I appreciate your frankness." Florence gave a sad little smile. "Even if it sounds like a brush off."

She leaned over and her lips pressed against mine.

"Time will tell, eh?"

"Get out here now, you two!" It was Jane's voice. "Quick! You *need* to see this."

I pulled myself upright with a groan and dropped through the hatch.

"It better be urgent," I snapped. "I was having a very important discussion."

I looked up at where the others were staring.

"Oh my God."

An enormous fireball was streaking across the sky, fiery tail billowing behind.

"It *can't* be."

"Elvis! Napoleon! Get Winston into the Carrier!" Jane sprinted for the vehicle. "It's a comet."

She paled visibly.

"I think it's *the* comet. The one that wiped everything out."

Winston moaned in pain as we carried him to the vehicle but didn't complain. As we bundled him inside, a blinding white light lit up the western horizon.

Jane took off at a ferocious speed, weaving between the rocks.

"We hit one of these and we're all going through what's left of the windshield," Elvis warned.

"They're thinning out and I'm not slowing down." Jane zig zagged, her face set in concentration. "Deal with it."

Then there were no more boulders and our speed crept up. Fifty, then sixty, then seventy miles an hour.

We heard the noise next. An ominous whooshing, punctuated with loud booms. Jane was hunched over the wheel, willing the craft to go faster.

"There! There!" George yelled down from the turret. "It's a time barrier!"

The iridescent curtain stretched ahead of us, tantalisingly close.

"Two more minutes!" Jane screamed. "We only need two more minutes!"

A wall of dust rose behind us, taller than any Tower. We saw the Triceratops herd whirling around, fifty feet up.

Then the blast hit.

The carrier was picked up and catapulted forwards. We clutched the sides of the craft and Elvis threw himself over Winston as we were swept through the dazzling barrier.

-Part 4-

How to start and control fire was probably the most significant human invention ever.

Craig A Lockard. *Societies, Networks and Transitions: A Global History*

-25-

We landed with a jolt and Winston screamed as Jane slammed on the brakes. Debris which had squeezed through the barrier with us bounced across the ground. A cloud of dust drifted away on the breeze.

"Wasn't there a saying once about women drivers?" He groaned, clutching his leg.

Florence administered more painkillers from the medical kit, while the rest of us got out and admired the view.

"This is a *distinct* improvement," Elvis said gratefully.

Lush green grass stretched as far as the eye could see, carpeting gently rolling hills. Florence sat Winston up so he could get a better look.

"I like it," he said bravely. "Makes me feel better already."

"You'll be right as rain before you know it." The girl felt his brow. "Your temperature's down and we have plenty of antibiotics."

"Great. Let's play tag."

"Any idea where we are?" I asked Jane.

"I've a feeling we're not in Kansas anymore."

"I'm sure that made some kind of sense to *you*."

George climbed back into the cab and checked the odometer.

"Distance-wise, we've driven over three thousand miles. It's taken the contents of the tank plus two drums of diesel to get here. We still have two left."

"I reckon that puts us somewhere in Eastern Europe," Florence said. "Or, maybe Asia."

"Wouldn't want to pin you down to something too specific." George started the engine. "Like an actual country."

"There are no countries, grumpy." The girl reached into the vehicle and hauled out a chunk of meat. "Let's have lunch. I rescued some of the T-Rex."

"This might sound stupid." Napoleon wiped grease from his chin. "But I keep wondering why a vehicle that was only supposed to make a trip to North Africa then back to New Hebrides is carrying so much fuel."

It was a question that had been niggling at me too. There was only one feasible explanation and I didn't like it one bit, which was why I'd kept my mouth shut. But Florence had obviously figured it out.

"Same reason five craft were sent on the mission," she said reluctantly. "When two would most likely have done. And why there were so few people on each."

"I don't get you." Napoleon looked at us quizzically.

"I'm betting Captain Jones had instructions to leave a couple of carriers with any group he found. Plus enough fuel, weapons and supplies to last a couple of years." She kicked a stone with her foot, avoiding the other's eyes. "With New Hebrides running out of recourses, the Town Council probably wanted to make peace with any Goners left alive in Pangea."

"*Why?*"

"I imagine they were considering abandoning the island and moving east."

There was a stunned silence. Our home was obviously closer to the end than anyone had thought.

"Aw, that's just dandy." Napoleon threw up his hands in despair.

"But he couldn't do it because only one vehicle survived the trip," I added. "And we managed to make the Pangeans hate us even more than they did before."

"What a screwup." Elvis sat down with a groan. "We're in the middle of nowhere and God knows the dangers we still face. And for what?" He angrily tore up a tuft of grass and let it blow away. "Let's be honest. What can we possibly achieve?"

"We're not clinging to some cliff face, hiding from dinosaurs." Jane put her arm around him and I felt a sudden twinge of jealousy. "At least we have somewhere to *go*."

"Do we?" George lay down resignedly, staring up at the fluffy clouds. "This vehicle will run out of fuel, eventually. How are we going to get from Asia to North America? Every jump we make forward in time, the continents separate more. We can't *swim* the gap."

"There was a land bridge between Siberia and Alaska until a few thousand years ago." Jane reached out and helped herself to another chunk of dinosaur. "Hopefully it'll still be there when we reach the end of this land mass."

"And if we run out of diesel before that?" George queried.

"We'll walk."

"Even Winston?" Napoleon glanced back at his friend.

I was as doubtful as everyone else, but I couldn't let them see it.

"If he's not healed by then, we'll damned well carry him." I clapped my hands together. "Let's get this show on the road. We're not beaten yet."

We drove by day and camped by night. This was by far the most pleasant leg of our journey, though not without incident. We gave a wide berth to a herd of mammoth grazing on a hillside and, one day, were stalked by a Sabre-Toothed Cat. But it was no dinosaur, and a few shots from our rifles saw it off. Unfortunately, a few rounds were all we could spare, for our small arms ammunition was dwindling too.

Elvis showed us how to make bows and arrows, so we began to hunt with those, becoming more accurate as we practised. We foraged for roots and berries and drank from streams that were fresh and clear.

At night we sat and talked. Learned to accept each other. George's abruptness became a source of amusement rather than irritation. Winston recovered his appetite. Even Jane thawed a bit, telling jokes and teaching me what she knew of earth's history, along with more quaint phrases and a couple of old-fashioned curses. Which she then forbade me to use. It was a lot to take in.

I tried to join their banter but found it increasingly difficult. How could I live in the moment when I was responsible for my companion's lives? I was the leader and this expedition was my idea. Could I keep them safe? How would we fare when the carrier eventually had to be abandoned?

What had I gotten us into?

Florence stayed by my side, offering me encouragement, but I pushed her away and retreated into my shell. She'd be better off with Elvis or

George, who were quietly resilient and hadn't let their own ambition get in the way of being decent human beings.

Then, one night, we met other people.

We were sitting round the fire, roasting deer over a spit, when we first became aware of them. A small group crouched in a nearby grove of trees, watching our every move.

They looked sort of like us, but darker. Closer to Winston's colour than mine. They wore only fur loincloths and their jaws were much larger than normal, jutting out like fleshy spades.

My hand immediately went for the nearest rifle.

"No." Winston pushed the gun away. "Can't you see they're more scared of us than the other way round."

"Speak for yourself."

But the boy struggled to his feet and hobbled towards the intruders, holding out a haunch of cooked meat.

"Winston, get back here," I hissed. "They have stone axes."

"Hey, guys." He ignored me. "Look what I got." He took a bite and rolled his eyes. "Mmmmm. Tasty!"

"I bet *you* look just as tasty to them." I slowly lifted the rifle. I hadn't forgotten the Pangean's dietary habits and these fellas looked too much like them for comfort.

"Let him try." Jane had the last blaster on her lap. "We can easily take them if they start to act threateningly."

The creatures backed away, keening to each other.

"Are they human?" I asked.

"Early ones, yes," Florence said. "Probably Homo Ergastar or Homo Erectus."

"Lost me there."

"Descendants of Homo Sapiens," she sighed. "That's you and me."

"Sorry if *I* haven't swallowed an encyclopaedia."

"Fat chance. You've never *even* seen one."

"Yes I have. It was full of fish."

"Ssssh." Elvis held up his hand. "They've stopped retreating."

The alpha male moved forward. Inch by inch, he approached Winston, baring teeth that looked like they could tear a man's arm off. My finger tightened round the trigger.

The male snatched the meat from George's hand and bit into it. His eyes lit up and he gave a broad smile. He passed the meat to his female companion and pulled the axe from his loincloth.

Jane raised the blaster.

Winston flinched but didn't move away.

The ape-man flipped the weapon in the air, caught it and held it out, handle first, to the boy.

"Much appreciated." He tucked the axe into his belt and indicated our little party. "You... eh... join us?" He pantomimed eating. "Have yum yums?"

Winston retreated towards us, beckoning the humanoids to follow. The male looked longingly at the deer roasting over our fire. Signalling for his troop to stay back, he crouched and weaved towards us, squinting his eyes against the glare of the flames.

"Stay very still," Winston warned. "We must look awful strange to him."

"*We* look strange?" George furrowed his brow. "*I* haven't got teeth like bricks."

The male approached Elvis and sniffed his neck.

"That tickles."

He repeated the process with each of us. We kept our heads bowed while he glanced uncertainly at his companions. Florence reached out slowly and offered him her dinner. The caveman crammed a chunk of venison into his mouth, swallowed it and gave a satisfied burp.

"You're welcome. Even if you niff like a sewage pipe."

Finally he signalled his troop. They loped over, ready to run or attack at the slightest provocation. I couldn't tell which.

Instead, they hunkered down a few feet away. Winston began to carve out pieces of venison with the stone axe and hand it to our strange guests, his movements slow and deliberate. Once they had eaten their fill, the humanoids inched closer to the flames and held out their hands.

"It's not the meat that's attracting them," Elvis whispered. "It's the fire. I don't think they've ever seen one under control before."

"I am Winston." The boy thumped his chest, and then pointed to the leader. "What is *your* name?"

"Mmmmmgh. Mmmmmgh."

"Well, hello Mmmmmgh." Winston held out his hand. "Pleased to meet you."

Mmmmmgh licked it. It seemed a friendly enough response, so I finally put down my rifle.

"We greet people like this." Winston gingerly lifted the caveman's hand and pressed the palm against his own. "It's how we say hello."

Mmmmmgh clasped the boy's hand and pumped it up and down, raising and lowering his eyebrows in time to the motion.

"Will you look at that!" Napoleon laughed. "The world's first handshake."

The cavemen and women roared with merriment, rocking back and forwards and making hooting noises. The lead male stared longingly at the fire, head tilted to one side.

"Haaargh. Haaargh."

"Let me show you something, guys." Winston began to pile dried brush and small twigs into a pile. He lifted the axe, then pointed to an identical weapon held by the smaller male.

"You... give... me... yours... too."

"Blark!" The creature clutched the precious possession to his chest.

"Nooo. Nooo." The lead male snatched the weapon from his companion and handed it to Winston.

"Don't worry, you'll get it back in a minute." The boy struck the two flint heads together, sending a shower of sparks over the kindling. Then he blew on it. The proto-humans leaned closer, transfixed by the display.

At the third try the brush caught fire. The tribe sat back on their haunches, eyes like marbles.

"Ohhhhhhhhh."

"That's how you make fire." Winston handed back the axes. "Simple really."

The cavemen thumped each other in excitement and two of the females scurried away, clonking the weapons together and chattering unintelligibly.

"That's right," Jane snorted. "Get your women to do the work."

The meal turned into a full-fledged party, even though our two groups couldn't talk to each other. In fact, the newcomers obviously hadn't mastered proper speech at all.

All the same, we had a ball. The caveman performed a dance for us, though they might have just been trying to dislodge fleas. They howled at the moon when it came up and we joined in. We showed them how to play rock, paper and scissors. They didn't understand, but it was fun watching them try.

Finally, we lay down together and went to sleep.

"They pong a bit," Winston said contentedly, as he drifted off. "But, to be honest, any company not trying to eat us is welcome."

I was still reserving judgement on that. The axes our guests sported weren't for decoration.

Finally, only the ape-man leader and I were left awake, eyeballing each other over the flames.

"Sorry, but I have to take the watch tonight," I explained, getting up and climbing into the carrier. "Keep away any bad animals. Plus, I don't really trust you not to slaughter us while we're out cold. Don't take it personally."

Mmmmmgh pointed to himself and scanned the horizon, one hand shielding his prominent brow.

"Yes. You have to watch *your* people. I understand."

And I did. I really did.

"You're a leader too."

I was woken by a hand slapping my cheek and my eyes shot open. Mmmmmgh was leaning over me, his troop bunched behind one hairy shoulder.

"Aaaaargh. Aaaaargh." He made clawing motions with his hands.

"Damn, I fell asleep." I sat up, wiping drool from the corner of my mouth. "What are you trying to say?

"Aaaaargh!" He bared his teeth.

"There's a predator nearby." Suddenly it was obvious. "Thank you for warning me."

Mmmmmgh clasped my hand and shook it. His mate held up two axes and slammed them together, sending up a shower of sparks.

"Oh yeah. Fire." I gave him a wink. "Glad we could be of help."

"Frrrrrrrrr. Frrrrrrrrrr."

And they loped off, waving as they went.

I watched until they were out of sight. But my heart was lifted in a way I couldn't even describe.

We were two tribes in the wilderness, separated by millennia, neither knowing what lay ahead. So what? I used to like surprises.

I jumped out of the carrier and pounced on the others, shaking them awake.

"Come on you dozy bunch." I stretched my arms wide, soaking up the rising sun. "Stop lazing about. We are heading round the *world*."

I took the first shift driving. The others had fallen back to sleep but Jane plonked herself down next to me.

"How come you're so cheerful this morning?" she asked, rubbing her eyes.

"I think I figured out what time period we're in."

"Really? Give it your best shot."

"When do you think humans first harnessed fire?" I asked.

"Nobody knows for sure," she replied. "About 500,000 years ago?"

"Then I reckon we're 500,000 years in the past."

"Wait… Are you saying what I think you're saying?"

"I am. You want proof this isn't a wasted trip?"

"We couldn't have…" She put a hand over her mouth.

"Girl. We gave these cavemen fire." I patted her cheek. "I'm willing to bet we just kick started civilization itself."

"I still haven't forgiven you entirely." Jane tentatively rested her head on my shoulder. "But I've lost the inclination to murder you."

She looked up at me.

"Unless you call me *girl* again."

"Sorry." I put my arm round her. It seemed like the natural thing to do and she didn't push me away.

I guess this was a day for making friends…

An hour later, we came to the next barrier.

-26-

It was bitterly cold in this new time period and the hilltops were covered in snow. An icy breeze soon woke the others up.

"We're definitely in Siberia now." George inspected the odometer. "Probably."

"Could be worse," Florence shivered. "Over the millennia ice ages came and went and this seems to be the end or beginning of one. If we'd arrived in the middle, we might have frozen to death."

I brooded at the wheel. Ice ages! How many hazards did the damned past hold? The girls had given me a crash course in pre-history but dangers I'd never considered kept cropping up.

At night, we slept in the carrier, the hoods of our sleeping bags pulled up, huddled together for warmth. There were still plenty of animals around and we existed mainly by hunting weird looking deer with unfeasibly large antlers. Our rifles were used as a last resort to protect us from carnivores and warn off bands of fur-clad hunters, who seemed to view the carrier as some kind of big game. They had prominent brows, deep-set eyes and long shaggy manes of hair.

"I presume they're Neanderthals." Jane watched a wary tribe through her binoculars. "They'll die out, eventually. Hopefully, before we do."

The truth was, we were becoming adept hunters ourselves. I suppose you learn fast when your very existence depends on acquiring new skills. Winston guarded the carrier while the rest of us stalked and killed our prey. We made spears and traps and our proficiency with bows and arrows had improved immensely. We skinned the animals, then cleaned the hides to make extra blankets and leg wraps. We dried and cured meat over the fire and fashioned knives from flint.

Days rolled by and the vehicle chugged east. The landscape remained unchanged and we were cold, miserable and wet most of the time. Winston, already weakened by his wound, suffered more than the rest of us.

When we finally came to the next time barrier the group gave a heartfelt cheer.

"Please let it be warmer," Napoleon clasped his hands together. "I haven't felt my feet for a week."

There was no need to discuss it further. I nodded and Florence drove through the wavering curtain.

We emerged into bright sunshine. Wildflowers studded the hillsides like a never ending quilt.

"Thank Heaven." Florence closed her eyes.

"Pretty cool." Napoleon roused Winston. "Looks like we missed the ice age after all."

We rested the whole day, enjoying the sun on our faces, then slept under the stars. Next morning Elvis opened the last diesel barrel.

"This will get us a couple of thousand miles more," he said. "After that, better start deciding what you want to carry."

I had already decided what *I* was going to carry. Winston Churchill. His leg was healing too slowly and walking any kind of distance would almost certainly re-open the wound. I was the biggest of the group and he weighed much less than me. Even so, I'd started doing push ups in preparation.

This was a much nicer landscape to travel across. We stuck to the foothills of a range of mountains, then entered a huge river and followed it for almost a week. George, who had taken over navigation duties, became increasingly frustrated.

"According to the odometer, we should have reached the end of the continent long ago and we're seriously low on fuel. Where's the ocean? We need to follow the coastline to find that land bridge, if it's even there."

Florence came and joined us.

"Rivers flow from higher ground to the sea, don't they?" she asked.

"That's right."

"So rivers in Asia should flow from the mountain regions *east*."

"I wish this one flowed east." Elvis steered round a rock. "We'd use up less diesel if we could go with the curr...."

He stopped in mid-sentence.

"Wait a minute. This river is flowing *west*."

"Took you a while," Florence grinned. "But you got there."

"Of course! We must have crossed the land bridge between Siberia and Alaska without even realising." I wasn't sure whether to be delighted or puzzled. "So, where are we?"

"The only waterway this big in Alaska is the Yukon, *assuming* the river systems are the same in this time period as they are in the 22nd century." Florence did a quick mental calculation. "If we've been following it for a week, we're probably already in Canada."

The other Goners punched the air and hugged each other.

"Head southeast." My heart leapt. "We're on the home straight, guys."

The next day, we saw several columns of smoke corkscrewing into the blue sky.

"Humans?" I asked Jane.

"Unless the Mammoths have learned to make fire." She steered the vehicle in the direction of the sooty tendrils. "Why don't we go look?"

"May as well," Elvis tapped the fuel gauge. "If they're unfriendly, we have just enough petrol to get away."

The hospitable landscape had given us a new-found enthusiasm and I felt a mounting excitement as we drove towards the smoke. It came from a small compound of circular stone huts. We parked and got out the binoculars. The inhabitants were dressed in fur but, apart from being bearded and long haired, they looked pretty much like us.

We left Winston in the vehicle and approached the village, keeping our guns lowered. We had also brought dried meat as a peace offering.

When they spotted us, the women scooped up their children and darted into the huts. The men, however, grabbed spears and advanced.

"Not too welcoming, are they?" Elvis slowed his pace.

"Give them a chance." Napoleon shouldered his rifle and held up both arms to show he was un-armed. "As far as they're concerned, we just turned up riding a dragon."

"Stay here." I pulled a chunk of dried meat from my bag and approached on my own, heart hammering in my chest.

Jane appeared beside me.

"What part of *stay* did you not understand?"

"I want them to see the women in this party are equal to the men." She elbowed me out of the way. "Besides, you still walk like a Regulator. You may as well wear a sign saying *I'm ready for a fight.*"

"I *am* ready. And these guys can't read, so it's just as well they know we mean business."

"Men," she grunted. "You can't resist a good war."

But no war was forthcoming. The tribesmen saw the meat and dropped their spears. One came forward and accepted my offering. And I had an ace up my sleeve.

I tipped the bag up and a dozen candy bars fell onto the grass.

"You been hiding these from us?" Jane squealed.

The truth was I *had* been hiding them. What could I say? I'm a sucker for sweeties. But I wasn't going to let Jane know that.

"Thought I'd need them for something just like this," I said disarmingly. "Besides, I didn't want you to ruin that great figure,"

"I have a great figure?" To my astonishment, she blushed. This girl was full of surprises.

The villager picked up a bar and held it under his nose.

"Smells good, huh?"

He stuffed it in his mouth.

"No, you're supposed to unwrap... Oh, never mind."

The villager spat out the paper and a look of sheer delight swept over his pitted face. He jabbered maniacally at his companions and they began to help themselves. Some broke chunks off and ran back to share the treat with their families. The leader marched up and gave me a bear hug. This guy didn't smell too bad, just a little smoky.

"I think we're safe," Jane laughed. "If you ask me, you just made some buddies for life."

That night we stayed in the village and the residents put on a celebration in our honour. They built a fire in the centre of the compound and sat around it yammering to each other and ogling us. I had no idea what they were saying but it was definitely a rudimentary language. Every now and then the women would come over and feel our clothing or run their fingers through our hair. Florence showed them how she cut hers with a knife and they set about grooming each other with gusto.

"Great. You just invented fashion and put the cause of feminism back a few thousand years," Jane scolded. "They'll be wearing high heels next."

"Stop being such a sourpuss." Florence sniggered. "Or I'll show them how to make mascara out of charcoal."

The next day we said our goodbyes and drove off. The villagers seemed genuinely sorry to see us go, though it was probably the candy bars they'd miss.

We only got a few miles when the engine spluttered and died. Napoleon twisted the key in the ignition, pumping the gas pedal.

Nothing.

The other's dismay was palpable. We all knew the carrier would eventually run out of fuel. Now it had actually happened, we were shell-shocked.

"Anyone want to get down and push?" Napoleon said in a small voice.

I knew I had to rally them, even though I felt like giving the vehicle a good kicking.

"It's not the end of the world, guys. That won't happen for a few thousand years." I jumped out of the carrier with a burst of false enthusiasm. "Grab what you can manage and we'll press on. Priority goes to medical supplies, sleeping bags and weapons. Don't forget the compass."

The others disembarked and began to push the essentials into their rucksacks.

"Winston, you walk until your leg gets too painful." I held out my hand to help him from the vehicle. "After that, I'll carry you on my back."

"No you won't." The boy folded his arms. "I'm not going."

"*Excuse* me?"

"We still have a huge distance to travel, John." Winston stood his ground. "You can't possibly lug me that far."

"Then we'll take turns." Napoleon came and stood beside him. "We're not leaving you behind."

"Oh yeah?" The boy's mouth tightened. "You're smaller than me and Florence and Jane weigh even less. It's physically impossible."

"We'll build some kind of stretcher to drag behind us," I insisted.

"It's called a travois. And it's usually pulled behind a horse, not a person."

"Not *helping*, Jane."

"I need to talk to you, John." Florence pulled me away from the group.

"Good." I leaned close to her ear. "Help me convince Winston not to be so pigheaded."

"Winston's *right*," she said wretchedly. "He's not going to make it in his state and neither are we if we have to carry him hundreds of miles."

"Florence!" I couldn't believe the most caring of our group was talking this way. "He's our *friend*."

"Which doesn't alter the facts."

"It's not an option!" I turned and shouted at the others. "You hear me? We'll wait until his leg heals."

"That could take months." Elvis stared at the ground.

"Then we'll *wait* months."

"John." Winston climbed slowly down from the carrier, grimacing in pain. "We don't know the perils ahead and, without the carrier, I'm a dead weight. A leader has to make tough decisions. Make this one."

"I already have." Sweat broke out on my forehead. "We're *not* leaving you alone."

"He won't be alone." Napoleon dropped his bag. "I'm staying as well."

"Are you *nuts*?"

"The village we just left will take us in." Napoleon put his arm around his friend's shoulders. "When Winston's well enough, we'll follow. I promise."

"No. No. No." I was on the verge of tears. "It's my job to look after you both."

"And you have." Winston limped over. "We know how to hunt and fight and live off the land." He grabbed me by the collar and pulled me down to his level.

"If you don't think you can save the human race," he hissed. "Be man enough to admit it. But

don't you *dare* use me as the reason for not trying."

I looked into his eyes. Saw only steely determination.

"All right." I ruffled his hair. "You and Napoleon come after us when you're well enough, all
right? I want you to promise me."

"You got it, boss."

"I'm not big on goodbyes." George strode over
and shook Napoleon and Winston's hands. "Let's
just say it's been a pleasure, despite the circumstances."

Elvis gave the boys our last two candy bars and
Jane and Florence hugged them both.

"Go on," Napoleon waved us away. "Get out of
here."

We picked up our packs and headed southeast.
Florence fell into step beside me.

"Don't look back, John. It'll only hurt more."

But I couldn't help it.

Napoleon Bonaparte was supporting Winston
Churchill as they hobbled back the way we had
come - two tiny figures dwarfed by a wilderness
they never asked to be in.

Deep in my heart, I knew I'd never see them
again.

-27-

We hiked over a range of enormous mountains, snow stinging our eyes, then descended onto a prairie that stretched as far as we could see. Eventually came to another time barrier. Moved through it without comment.

Funny how you get used to things.

But I couldn't get used to not having Napoleon and Winston around. I'd hardly spoken for days. It wasn't my companions' fault and they were obviously as upset as me. But I was Alan Carver, and I had failed to save all of *my* people.

I finally knew how he felt.

A week later, we came to another shimmering curtain.

"I didn't think we'd travelled *that* far," Elvis remarked.

We cautiously ventured through the barrier, only too aware how vulnerable we had become without the carrier.

The landscape was almost identical on the other side.

"The rifts are coming closer together and I don't think the historical periods are nearly as long either. It's like time is accelerating the farther we travel." George pulled the modern map of the world from his bag and spread it on the grass. "I reckon the landscape is pretty much the same now as it will be in the 22nd century."

"Any idea of our location?" I roused myself long enough to feign interest.

"The mountains we crossed stretch north to south, so I'm betting they're the Rockies." George ran his finger down the map. "Which would put us in British Columbia or even Montana."

"Let's camp here, then. It's getting late."

We found a promising site near a stream and settled down for the night.

"We're going to collect some water and see if we can snag a couple of trout." Jane and Florence picked up our canteens. "Want to come George?"

"I'm fine."

"We'd feel safer with you along." Florence shot him a winning smile.

"Oh. You got it."

As soon as they had left, Elvis came and sat next to me.

"They leave so you could give me a lecture?" I glared into the fire.

"You have to snap out of it, John." He handed me a strip of dried meat and a handful of berries. "Everyone is worried."

"I'm getting you there, aren't I?"

"The rest of us are trying to make the best of a bad situation."

"Bully for you."

"They were our buddies too," Elvis said patiently. "We're the ones who ganged up to leave them behind."

"That supposed to make me feel better?"

"It should. We tried to take the pressure off you. And now you're punishing us for it." He moved to the other side of the fire. "You're acting like a selfish ass."

I knew that and it only put me in a blacker mood.

I lay looking up at the stars long after the others had fallen asleep. Elvis was right, of course. I'd let them make the hard decision about Winston when it should have been my job to insist he be left behind. I was afraid they'd hate me for it and now they blamed me for blaming them. Or something like that.

All right. I'd tried being Alan Carver and it had backfired. From now on, I was back to be John Wayne again. No more tantrums. No more black moods. No more backing down.

No more caring.

The next day I saw a dark blot on the landscape. We crawled onto a small bluff and got out the binoculars.

It was a jumble of triangular tents next to a bunch of funny looking animals penned in by brush fences. I handed the binoculars to Florence.

"A Native American village, by the look of it," she said. "They used to be named Indians, the tents are called tepees and they've got a corral of horses."

Even I knew what a horse was for.

"We're going down there." I stood up and shouldered my pack. "Get your weapons ready."

"Our ammo is real low and we've got no vehicle to protect us." Elvis looked doubtful. "Are you sure that's a good idea?"

I remembered my resolution from the night before.

"We need those horses to cover ground more efficiently."

"None of us know how to ride, John. Or even *seen* a horse before."

"We didn't know how to use a bow and arrow or trap or hunt before." I strode purposefully towards the village. "We'll learn."

The natives came out to meet us. They were tall and tanned, dressed in buckskin and carrying bows and arrows of their own.

"Keep your hands where these savages can see them," I ordered. "If any of them makes a threatening move, go for your guns."

My companions looked at me in consternation.

"I'm not losing anyone else. Got it?"

The Indians stopped when they saw George Custer and began to yammer excitedly. One brave approached the boy and gently touched his platinum locks.

"Graham!" He smiled broadly at his party. "Hakakta Graham."

"It hasn't been washed for a while." George jerked his head away. "Make a terrible scalp."

"Hiyu, Graham." The leader beckoned for us to follow.

"Actually my name is…"

"Don't tell him!" Florence shook her head urgently. "Not yet."

"Ok." George looked puzzled. "Whatever you say."

Our group marched into the village, Indians on all sides, gawping and gesturing. The lead brave led us to a tepee on the outskirts and motioned to stop.

"Hau Graham!" he shouted, slapping the tent. "Uma. Uma!"

The flap opened and a man stepped out. He, too, was dressed in buckskin, but there the resemblance with the Indians ended. For a start, he was white, with bushy blonde hair and matching eyebrows.

"What's aw the fuss aboot, Red Dog?" He stopped in his tracks when he saw us. "What in the name o God?"

"You speak English," I gasped.

"I speak Scottish, wee man." The stranger retorted. "And though my Lakota is poor, it suffices for day-to-day intercourse with these fine fellows."

He clapped the Indian brave on the arm.

"Lila Pilamayaye, Red Dog. I'd like a word with these folk. In private, if you dinnae mind."

"Takuye, Graham?"

"Ha, Red Dog. Takuye." He winked at George. "Takuye means relative. They think we must be kin, blondie, on account o yer bonny hair."

"If it stops my hair ending up on a pole, you can call me your long lost auntie."

"Just nip inside." The man held the flap open. "I'm the only white man they've ever seen. Got yerselves oot o sight before they decide it's an invasion."

I ducked into the tepee. It was smoky and smelly and I coughed loudly, wafting the air with one hand, letting my vision adjust to the poor light.

"Wooooah!" I covered my eyes. "I'm *so* sorry."

There was a naked woman in the corner, clutching a blanket to her chest.

"Walks with the Rain." The man clasped his hands together and bowed respectfully. "Could you give us a wee minute? Iyokipe? The wee ones are no quite ready to see sic a fine sight."

"Of course, Graham." The woman wrapped the rug around her slender body as she stood. She giggled and pinched George's cheek on the way out.

"Takuye?"

"Apparently, we're distant cousins." George's eyes were almost on stalks.

The stranger motioned for us to sit.

"Angus Graham, at your service." He shook our hands in turn. "Formerly of Edinburgh, Scotland and a deserter from his majesty's armed forces, I'm no ashamed tae say." He leaned back and lit a pipe, adding to the fug filling the already opaque interior. "Now, who the devil might *you* be?"

I glanced at Jane for help. Could almost see her mind whirring.

"We got separated from our parents," she began. "They were part of a wagon train crossing the plains…"

"Nonsense, lassie." Alan Graham cut her off with a slice of his hand. "There's no another paleface within a thousand miles o this place. I never even heard of a wagon train."

"You're obviously a plain speaking man," I interrupted. "May I talk frankly too?"

"I'd prefer it."

"My people need to rest and we've run out of food." I hesitated. "We'd also like horses and to be taught how to ride them."

"No too demanding, then." Graham took an enormous drag on his pipe and breathed out a plume of dirty grey smoke. "Horses are like gold around here, as ye surely ken. What have ye got to trade?"

"Weapons. Weapons like you've never seen."

"I've used muskets before, wee man. I was in the army." He nodded at my rifle. "Though never one that fancy, I'll freely admit."

He sniffed disdainfully.

"Pah. A gun is no worth a horse to *these* people."

"It's more than a musket." I retorted. "Care for a demonstration?"

"Aye. But it's best my hosts bear witness too. It's their herd." Alan Graham got to his feet. "They're an inquisitive people an probably aw still standing outside."

He was right. When we emerged from the tepee, blinking in the sunlight, a murmur rose from the gathered crowd.

"Florence? Give me your blaster."

"It's only got a couple of charges left," she warned, handing it over.

"It's important." I aimed at a large boulder a hundred feet away.

"This isn't some kind of sacred object is it?" I thought I better check.

"It's a *rock*, laddie."

"Good." I sighted and fired. The boulder disintegrated, condensing into a ball of smouldering ash.

You could have heard a pin drop.

"Whit infernal device am I witnessing?" Alan backed away from us. "Is this witchcraft?"

"No, it's just a really cool gun." It was my turn to be condescending. "If I was a witch, I'd be waving my arms around and muttering spells. Jeez. What year *is* this?"

"*Whit*? It's 1715."

"That explains a lot."

"Who the blazes are ye?" Alan couldn't take his eyes off the blaster. He licked his lips hungrily. "Where did ye get those?"

"Does it matter?" I handed him the weapon to inspect. "If your companions teach us to ride and give us horses, we'll show you how to use these and leave them behind when we go."

I remembered Captain Jones making the same deal with the Pangeans. And look how *that* turned out.

Alan began to talk to the Lakota in their own language. They looked fearfully at us and nodded.

"You can have anything ye want," he said finally. "They think you're some kind o Gods."

"That's very flattering, but we're not. Honest."

"I know *that*," The Scotsman guffawed. "I gave up believing in the Lord when my family was killed in the great pestilence back hame."

"I'm sorry."

"Whit's done is done." He put his arm around me. "But you're now honoured guests. Make the most of it."

He leaned forward and whispered roguishly in my ear.

"I certainly do."

Unlike the Pangeans, the Indians were as good as their word. We soon mastered the rudiments of bare backed riding and the natives made us deer-skin clothes to match their own. Just in time, too, for our home-made fur outfits were falling apart.

To be honest, we thoroughly enjoyed our stay. George Custer in particular, as his blonde curls were a constant source of fascination for the ebony haired natives. The girls, especially, seemed to like it.

After a few weeks, we were refreshed and ready to go, much to his annoyance.

"Couldn't we wait another couple of days?" he pleaded.

"Sure. What's the fate of the human race compared to you being able to chase a bit of skirt?"

Jane put hands on her hips. "Get your gear together, Casanova."

Alan Graham rode with us to the river's edge.

"I'll take my leave of you, noo." He reigned in his mount. "I still dinnae ken who ye are, but I wish you every success in your endeavours."

"You too, Alan." I made to hand over the weapons. "Here you go. Deal's a deal."

"I dinnae want them."

"*What*?"

"These are a fine and noble people." He looked sadly back at the village. "Civilization will catch up tae their wee paradise soon enough, and it will destroy them, if I'm any judge o human nature."

He stroked his horse's mane.

"I see nae need tae speed up that process."

"But they expect the weapons. You'll be an outcast if you don't deliver."

"I sense ye know how *exactly* how that feels." Graham's eyes grew steely. "I wis a man who lived by the sword and led many comrades tae their deaths, besides. I'd rather these people ordered my banishment than became like me."

His message couldn't have been plainer.

"Farewell to ye." He wheeled his steed around. "I mean nae disrespect, but I hope fervently never tae see yir like again."

Then he galloped off.

-28-

I loved horse riding. The sheer power of the animal under me was exhilarating and it was much easier to hunt when we could actually keep up with our prey. Best of all, the pounding of hooves and the whistling wind blanked out my thoughts.

At nights I still sat on my own and the others had given up trying to engage me in conversation. It wasn't that I didn't want to talk, I just couldn't afford to let them get too close. Who knew what terrible decisions I'd have to make in the future? Whatever they were, I couldn't let my companions be tainted by them.

We arrived at the next barrier and reigned in our mounts.

"Leave the compass here." I pulled the binoculars from my neck and dropped them on the ground. Then I remembered Alan's warning

"And bury the blasters. They're spent anyway."

"Are you sure?" George asked.

"These objects are from the 22nd century and, from now on, I think we'll need to blend in. We can ask directions to get where we're going."

I might have thought that through a bit more.

Within hours we came to a wooden, hand painted sign.

Madison. Dakota Territory. Population 700.

"From now on, you follow my lead and do exactly as I say." In the distance were a bunch of ramshackle clapboard buildings lining a grubby main street. On the hill beyond were more wooden houses and a small cemetery. "I want your word on this."

"Why? What are you up to?" Jane tugged at her fringed jacket. "And I don't know if this is the best attire to be wearing going into what's obviously a frontier town."

"Unless you want to make an entrance naked, we're stuck with what we've got. Your word."

"I trust you," Florence piped up. The others didn't seem so convinced.

And what an entrance we made. Women fairly sprinted for cover, holding their bustled skirts out of the mud. Men emerged instead, clutching rifles and revolvers.

I guess people never really change.

"Boy, we really are in the wild west," Florence whispered, as we dismounted.

"Wild?" Elvis stood protectively in front of her. "They look bloody manic."

"Stop right there," A man wearing a sheriff's badge emerged from the crowd and waved the throng back. He was wearing a black waistcoat, black hat and a white, sweat-stained shirt.

"Perhaps you'd care to explain to these terrified folk how three white children can come riding right outta Indian territory, an dressed like savages to boot?"

He tilted his hat back.

"You *are* white, aintcha?"

"You ever see an Indian with blond hair?" George pointed to his head. "And they're not terrified, just armed to the nines. *We're* the ones who are terrified."

"Don't you sass me, son," the sheriff snapped. "What's your name?"

George glanced at Florence.

"You can tell him."

"George Custer."

There was a ripple of laughter from the citizens.

"Named after our famous general, hero of the Battle of Wasita River, huh?" The sheriff chuckled. "Yet here you are, dressed like some murdering Redskin."

"Wasn't that a massacre, rather than a battle?" Jane shot back. "Didn't he kill mainly women and children?"

"Shut *up*, Jane." Elvis hissed through clenched teeth.

It was too late. The crowd's good humour vanished.

"*That's* the person I'm named after?" George paled. "Why didn't you *tell* me?"

"Not the time to thrash this out, buddy." I raised my hands. "My name is John Wayne. My companions and I have no weapons, sir, and we came looking for sanctuary."

"Explain."

"We were separated from our wagon train and captured by the Lakota." I recalled Jane's previous excuse. "We been with them about six months but managed to escape while they were asleep. We survived by hiding during the day and travelling at night."

"How do we know they ain't spies?" one burly cowboy yelled.

"How could you say that?" Jane burst into tears. "You don't know what we've been through."

Seizing her cue, Florence broke down in a fit of sobbing. A stout woman in a bustled dress surged out of the crowd and threw her arms round the girl.

"You leave those young 'uns alone," she chastised. "God knows what the ungodly heathens did to 'em."

Florence gave me a quick thumbs-up behind the woman's back.

"They still following you?" The sheriff asked.

"Yeah. About fifteen of them, as far as I can tell," I lied. "They turned back when they saw we were going to reach the town."

"Those creatures are *here*?" The lawman's hand went instinctively to his gun. "Miss Rocca, see if you can rustle up these kids some decent civilized clothes, then send 'em to the deputy. The rest of you? I want every available person on horseback in ten minutes. We'll teach those redskins a lesson they ain't never going to forget."

There was no shortage of volunteers.

Mrs Rocca sat us round her kitchen table and cooked a meal. Actually, it was more like a banquet. There were foodstuffs I didn't even know existed, never mind eaten. Ham and eggs. Steak and beans. Sourdough bread. Corn and grits.

It was absolutely delicious.

"Tuck in, youngsters," our host beamed. "You probably haven't had a decent meal in a good while."

"About 150 million years," Elvis agreed, through a mouthful of fried potatoes. Mrs Rocca frowned at him.

"That boy ain't right in the head, is he?"

After we were finished, Mrs Rocca showed us into a guest room, then came back with an armful of clothes.

"You girls can have my son, Billy's cast-offs." She dumped the pile on the bed. "It ain't exactly feminine attire, I'm afraid."

"That's OK," Jane said quickly. "I'm not really keen on wearing a skirt."

"I aint got nothin your size." She smiled apologetically at George.

"I'll live."

"But you fine strapping lads can have my husband's stuff." She sized up Elvis and myself. "He was a small man, but he could fell a steer just by buttin heads with it."

"Won't *he* be wanting them?" I inquired politely.

"My husband and son died in a Cheyenne raid back in 1866."

I didn't know what to say about that.

Mum and dad were right. The olden days really were a bit crap.

We made our way over to the jailhouse. Now that most of us were dressed like proper cowboys, nobody paid much attention, though George's buckskins still drew a few raised eyebrows.

The deputy was a huge man, most of it stomach, with a handlebar moustache and sideburns curling down over his peppery chin.

"Come in kids." He padded back to his desk. "Want some coffee? It's fresh brewed."

"What's coffee?" I asked Jane.

"Some kind of brown stuff they used to drink."

"Sure. I'd love some."

"I just need to get things straight for when the sheriff comes back." He poured us each a tin mug and handed them out. "Tell me everything that happened to ya."

I took a sip of the hot liquid and sprayed it across the room.

"Ack… Ack… Euuuugh!"

"It *is* pretty strong." The deputy fetched a pencil and sat at the desk.

"Who's that?" George asked.

The back of the jailhouse consisted of two cells. One was empty and the other contained a Native American girl about our age, crouching on the bed. She was pretty but painfully thin and a deer hide dress hung loosely on her emaciated body. A line of dried blood descended from the corner of her mouth.

"Picked her up outside town a couple of days ago." The deputy licked his pencil. "Claims she's from the Williams Reservation."

"I *am* from the reservation," the girl spat.

"Then you should have *stayed* there." The lawman curled his lip disdainfully. "You ain't allowed off."

George moved forwards and gripped the bars, looking intently at her.

"My family have no food." She climbed off the bed and faced the boy. "I was taught English by missionaries, so I came to beg for something to eat."

A tear ran down her cheek.

"We are not part of the raiding parties. We did as you asked and moved to a terrible place, with no buffalo and no good grass. Now we are starving."

"Aint that a shame." The deputy turned back to us and lowered his voice. "If I had my way, I'd exterminate the lot of 'em."

"Why are you fighting each other?" Elvis took a tentative sip of his coffee. "Isn't the land big enough for all of you?"

"They found *gold* in the Black Hills, boy." The deputy rubbed two fingers together. "It's in Indian territory an those critters don't even know what to do with it."

He gave a wolfish smile.

"There's five bags o gold dust sittin in the bank right now as proof, an plenty more where it came from."

That got my attention.

"Word is, General Custer's 7th Cavalry an General Crook's forces are heading up towards The Little Big Horn to surprise a big Sioux village." The lawman continued. "That should knock the fight outta them."

George closed his eyes at the mention of his namesake and gripped the bars harder. The girl lay back down on the bed and curled into a ball.

"They're going to wipe those filthy monsters off God's earth." The deputy took a slurp of coffee and smacked his lips.

"If it's a village, won't there be women there?" Florence said in a shocked voice. "And children?"

"For sure, missie. But nits grow into lice."

George whirled and stepped behind him. He raised his arm and brought the side of his palm down on the man's neck. The deputy gave a grunt and toppled off his chair, unconscious before he hit the dusty floor.

"What the hell are you doing?" I gasped.

"Time we parted ways, guys." George pulled a pair of gun belts from the wall and began strapping them on. "You want to carry further on into *civilization*, go ahead. I've been here an hour and I'm already sick of it."

He took down a pistol, twirled it expertly around one finger and slammed the weapon into the holster at his side.

"I'm going back."

"The battle of the Little Big Horn was in 1876." Jane knelt over the fallen lawman to make sure he was still alive. "Think it through, will you? We passed through a barrier. The Lakota we stayed with have been dead for over a century and a half."

"Then I'll find their ancestors." George picked up a shotgun. Within seconds he had figured out how it worked and was loading it with shells. The rest of us watched in shocked silence. "This is *their* land and we owe them our lives."

"You're white, there's a war on and you're called George Custer." I scratched my cheek awkwardly. "They, eh… might not be too pleased to see you."

"Take me along." The girl in the cell leapt up and reached through the bars. "I will tell the Lakota Sioux of these deeds. They will accept you."

"Especially if I warn them the 7th Cavalry is coming." George fished a set of keys from the deputy's belt and unlocked the cell door. "Don't worry. You're safe with me."

He smiled gently at the girl.

"What are you called?"

"Angpetu. In your language it means Radiant Sky."

"I'm George... eh… Custer."

"Your mean-looking friend is right." The girl smiled wanly. "This is not a good name."

"Mean looking!" I couldn't believe my ears. Florence hid a smile.

"I shall call you Hota," Angpetu continued. "It is Sioux for white."

"That'll do." George returned to the guns, taking down another two revolvers and tucking them into his shirt.

"Enough!" Elvis exploded. "For God's sake talk some sense into him, John."

"All right, George." I caught his arm. "I admit New Hebrides never did anything for you. But you can't just abandon your friends."

"I imagine that posse will be on its way back, having discovered there's no Indians chasing us." George took down a rifle and tossed it to Radiant Sky. "They're scared and suspicious. You're going to end up in those cells unless I create a diversion that allows you to get away."

"You're fourteen and the townspeople are ready to shoot anything that moves," I countered. "You won't stand a chance."

"Really? I was trained to fight from the day I was born." George waved off my objections. "Don't worry, I won't kill any of them." He glanced at Radiant Sky. "Neither must you, Angpetu."

"If that is what you wish."

"This is insane!" Elvis threw his hands in the air. "We can't just leave you."

They all looked at me. I hesitated, then remembered what Alan Graham had said to me. It *was* my job to make the hard decisions.

"Everyone grab weapons." I took down a gun for myself. "What's your plan buddy?"

"No plan. I'm going straight up the main street and steal a couple of horses from outside the saloon. That ought to attract the townsfolk's attention."

"Ya *think*?"

"The rest of you skirt round the back to the livery stables. Grab your mounts and head east. I'll go west." He looked down at his buckskins. "I'm pretty certain they'll come after *me*."

"You can't let him…" Elvis began.

"I said *arm* yourselves." I slammed my hand on the desk. "He's giving us a chance and we're taking it."

I took the boy by the shoulders.

"You stay well… Hota."

"I hope you manage to save New Hebrides." George clasped me back. "But part of me doesn't really care. I've found where I belong."

He held out his hand and Radiant Sky took it.

"You trust me to get you out safely?"

"I do."

"Then let's go." He gathered the others together and hugged them.

"No goodbyes." He kissed Florence gallantly on the back of her hand. "I'm not big on goodbyes."

He cocked the shotgun and stepped out of the jailhouse door.

"Take the rest of the weapons and lock them in one cell. Put the deputy in the other." I went to the window and peered through the drapes at George strolling confidently up the main street.

"He'll never make it," Elvis groaned.

"Yes, he will." Jane smiled softly. "Because the Sioux village *wasn't* surprised by General Custer.

In fact, they massacred the 7th Cavalry at the battle of Little Big Horn. Thanks to *this* George Custer, I presume. He must have warned them after all."

"Wow," Florence whistled. "That's a bit ironic."

"Florence and Jane? Go round the back of the town to the livery stable and saddle the horses. My butt's sore from riding bareback." I let the drapes fall back into place. "Wait a few minutes, then bring them round to the rear of the bank."

"What will I do?" Elvis asked.

"Wait until George and Radiant Sky are on horseback, then go out and start shooting at them."

"*What?*"

"I want you to *miss*, don't worry. Just follow my lead." I picked up a huge blade from the desk. "What on earth is this?"

"It's called a Bowie Knife," Florence and Jane had finished dragging the lawman's bulky body across the floor and into the cell.

"Way cooler than a baton." I shoved the knife up my sleeve. "Listen, we're going to need money where we're going."

I gave a grin.

"So, while the rest of the townspeople go after George, we're going to rob the bank."

Custer was certainly a cool customer. He sauntered up the street to the saloon, staring down anyone who seemed too curious. While he had the townspeople's undivided attention, Florence and Jane slipped out of the jailhouse and round the back of the houses.

George reached the saloon before anyone challenged him.

"Where you goin with that injun?" A grizzled old prospector blocked his path. "She's supposed to be in jail."

The boy didn't even slow down. He lashed out, fingers straight. The man went down, clutching his throat and making strangled gasps. George nodded to Radiant Sky, who began to untether two horses from the saloon rail.

A bullet whistled past her head and she ducked but kept at it. George turned and fired his revolver twice in rapid succession. Two cowboys retreated, holding their wrists and howling in pain. Radiant Sky freed the horses as the boy raised his shotgun and blew the bat-wing doors of the saloon off their hinges. There was pandemonium inside as the occupants dived for cover.

The boy dropped his shotgun and spun in an arc, fanning the hammer of his revolver with the palm of one hand. Windows exploded, barrels sprang leaks and Stetsons flew off the heads of astonished onlookers.

Within seconds, the dusty street was deserted.

George and his new companion leapt onto the horses and galloped out of town. Radiant Sky kept her head down but George held the reins in his teeth, firing as he went.

"Now!" I pushed Elvis out the door. We ran up the main street, shooting over the heads of the retreating figures. A few men emerged from the clapboard houses again and ran towards us.

"He's gone native," I groaned, sinking to my knees. "He knocked out the deputy and hit me on the head with a rifle butt when I tried to stop him."

"Let's get you to sawbones, son." One man knelt beside me.

"Tell me where the doctor is and I'll fetch him." Elvis picked up his cue. "You got to stop that crazy fool. He's going to warn the Indians about General Custer!"

That caused a rare old pandemonium. Within minutes the saloon was empty and another posse was galloping out of town, following George's trail of dust.

Elvis and I headed in the direction of the doctor's house but ducked into the bank before we got there, pulling neckerchiefs over our faces. Inside was one teller with owlish glasses and a male and female waiting to be served. I drew my pistol and pointed it at the clerk's head.

"Open the safe right now and give me the bags of gold inside."

"I ain't got the combination."

"Yes you do. You're the only staff here."

"If you kill me, you'll never know what it is."

Jeez. I hoped the bank was paying this guy a lot of money. He should certainly be up for employee of the month.

"Cover him," I barked at Elvis. I pulled the Bowie knife from my sleeve and stepped behind the male customer.

We Regulators are taught a cool trick – how to disable someone by pinching a nerve in their neck. Elvis knew this. The teller didn't.

I thrust the knife into the customer's coat, just missing his body. At the same time, I squeezed the base of his neck. He dropped to the floor and the woman gave a whimper of terror.

"Aw, John!" Elvis played along, rolling his eyes at the clerk. "I tell you, that guy is plumb kill-crazy!"

The teller began to shake.

"Open the safe or the woman's next."

"All right! All right!" He scrambled to get out the gold.

"Sorry Ma'am," I whispered while his back was turned. "Got no intention of harming you and the guy on the floor's just out cold."

"No need to apologise," she smiled wanly. "They was gonna foreclose on my homestead."

"Then tell everyone we headed west." To her delight, I poured some of the dust into her purse.

We emerged from the bank with two bags each and raced round the back of the building. Florence and Jane were waiting for us.

"I've decided life on the open range isn't for me." I dumped the gold into our saddlebags and swung onto my mount.

"But, boy, I *do* like eggs."

-30-

We rode our mounts at full speed until we reached the next barrier, only stopping to shoot and cook a couple of jackrabbits on the way. When we finally arrived, the muzzles of our horses were flecked with spittle and waves of musty steam rose from their trembling flanks. To the north, we could see a huge lake sparkling in the sunlight, a large grimy town ringing its shore.

"That's probably Cleveland, Ohio." Florence looked at a battered map she had lifted from the jailhouse. "Even in the 19th century, it was pretty big."

"Leave the horses. This area will be heavily populated in the future." Jane gave a wry smile. "If we leap forward into someone's sitting room, it's probably best not to be mounted."

"Shame, really." I mentally pictured the scene. "That'd be pretty funny."

"Not for the family living there."

"We keep the weapons, though." I wasn't about to give up my revolver. "In case we jump right into the Great Chaos."

"We won't." Florence patted her horse's neck. "I figured out the whole thing while we were riding."

"Say *what*, now?"

"Jurassic period. 150 million years ago. End of the Cretaceous, 65 million years ago. Then we ended up 500,000 years in the past." The girl counted off time periods on her fingers. "We crossed a land bridge between ice ages, which must have been about 12,000 years BC. Those dates are huge approximations but I memorised the exact mileage on the carrier, so I know the spatial coordinates and can do a rough calculation."

"Are you making this *up*?"

Jane waved at me to be quiet and let Florence continue.

"After that, I had to work out distances by calculating the rough speed of the horses over the time travelled, but I know the *exact* dates of the last two time periods - 1705 and 1886." Florence smiled brightly. "It's enough to produce a formula to calculate when we end up next."

"And that would be?"

"1976."

"You have *got* to be kidding me. There's no way you can do that!"

"All right," the girl admitted. "It might be 1975."

The rest of us gaped at her.

"I knew you were smart," Elvis stammered. "But I didn't know you were *that* smart."

"I don't like to show off." Florence blushed.

We came out of the other side of the barrier in a cramped alleyway lit by electric street lamps. Strings of clothes were draped on washing lines from window to window, flapping like ghosts in the moonlight.

"Should we steal some of those?" Elvis pointed up. "Try to blend in again?"

"We're wearing jeans, cowboy boots and checked shirts." Jane shook her head. "Give them a wash and I bet they'll do fine." She felt in her pockets. "We need modern money, though. Can't hunt in the city."

"We've got gold." Elvis reminded us. "I doubt it's normal currency around here, but it's probably worth a fair bit."

"We could always use this." I patted my colt. "I quite enjoyed bank robbing."

"Let's not start our first night in civilization as villains, huh?" Jane snatched the gun away. "Why don't we sell the weapons before you shoot some old lady for her life savings?"

"Only the rifles." Elvis pulled a sheet down from the washing line and wrapped our carbines in it. "I'm not parting with the small arms."

It looked to be a pretty rough neighbourhood, but we'd been in far more dangerous situations. Despite the fact that we were dressed like out-of-town hicks, our hollow eyes and defiant walk discouraged anyone from approaching. We waited until the sun had risen, then found a pawn shop, one window shuttered and covered in graffiti.

Florence and I walked in and laid the rifles on the counter. A small, hunched man shuffled out from the back and did a double-take when he saw the weapons. Florence didn't give him the chance to recover from his shock.

"We got a Springfield, a Sharps and a Winchester - all antiques in pristine condition," she said. "I want $500 for the lot. No questions asked."

The man inspected them, then looked warily at us.

"Very nice. How old are you kids?"

"That's a question."

"I could get into a lot of trouble buying weapons from a couple of teenagers." The man's fingers crept towards one of the guns. "They got to be stolen."

"*They're* not loaded." I pulled up my shirt to reveal a revolver tucked into my waistband. "This one is."

"Okay, okay…" He retreated, holding up his palms.

"Let's not resort to unpleasantness." Florence pulled a canvas bag from her rucksack and opened it on the counter. A pile of gold dust glittered under the strip light. "What if we threw in an incentive?"

"Oh!" The exclamation caught in the shopkeeper's throat. "Where did you *get* this?"

"It's gold." I pressed home our advantage. "You have two minutes to check it. Then we take our trade somewhere else."

"I recognise gold when I see it." The man wiped his mouth with the back of one liver-spotted hand. "How do I know you aint operating a sting for the cops?"

"Because, as you pointed out, we're kids." I folded up the bag. "C'mon Florence. This guy's a pussy."

I grinned from ear to ear. Finally got to use one of Jane's cuss words.

"I'll give you $2,000 for the lot," the pawnbroker blurted out. "It's all I got in the shop."

"You ripping us off, old man?" I pulled up my shirt again.

"My friend is a suspicious type." Florence pulled me back. "But he's probably right. Make it $3,000 and you'll never see us again."

Elvis and Jane met us outside.

"We have cash." I held up a wad of notes triumphantly. "Gold is worth a *lot*."

"Put it away," Jane admonished. "By the looks of this area, there are guys on these streets who'd kill their own grandmother for that kind of money."

"By the way, we asked the shopkeeper and Florence was completely wrong." I patted my companion's cheek. "It's only 1974."

"Let's go and get somewhere to sleep," Jane yawned. "I'm dead on my feet."

There was no point in going to a nice hotel. Nobody there would rent a room to a bunch of kids. Instead, we picked the nastiest fleapit we could find. The guy behind the counter had his legs draped across the desk, flicking through a magazine that appeared to have a naked woman on the cover.

Maybe reading wasn't such a bad thing after all.

Above him was a sign saying Rooms $12.00 per night.

"I'd like two adjoining suites, my good fellow." I jerked a thumb at Elvis. "One for us and one for the ladies."

"Beat it." The clerk barely glanced at us. "No under-agers."

"Get your feet off that desk when you talk to me."

"Huh?" The man put down his magazine and slowly stood. His muscled torso was covered in some kind of drawings and he placed huge palms on the counter, leaning forwards until his face was inches from mine. "*What* did you just say?"

Jane plunged a knife into the wood between his outstretched fingers. He jerked his hand back with a girlish squeal.

"Two rooms cost $24.00." She pulled the knife out and began to pare her nails with it. "We'll give you $100 for each night we stay. What you do with the rest of the dough is up to you."

"But if you call the Lawmen," Elvis added. "You'll find that blade in your inky chest."

The Goners stared at him. We had dark circles under our eyes and dust matted our clothes. My hand crept towards the colt hidden under my shirt. It was a move I'm sure he'd seen before.

"Rooms 26 and 27." The attendant pulled two keys from a hook above his head. "We get raided by the cops occasionally. If it happens, use the fire escape."

We went back out, bought Pizza, Coke, fries and a newspaper, then took them back to our room. The clerk had his feet on the desk again and didn't even acknowledge us.

After we had bathed, we put our clothes in the bath and soaked them, while we sat around wrapped in threadbare towels.

"This is the finest thing I've *ever* tasted." Elvis wolfed down another slice of Pizza. "I don't know what Pepperoni's made of, but I could eat it for the rest of my life."

"This Coke stuff makes you burp." Florence let out a belch that almost rattled the walls. "Isn't it an illegal drug?"

"We need to talk guys." Jane put down her slice.

I knew what was coming.

"We're nearly at the end of our road and we still don't have a strategy."

And there it was. The thing we'd all been afraid of admitting. What we'd achieved was nothing short of astonishing. But where did we go from here?

"According to my calculations," Florence said. "The next barrier will send us right into the middle of the Great Chaos."

"I don't see how we can even survive it." Jane curled shapely legs up under her body. "Never mind change anything."

"Are you saying we should stay here?" Elvis helped himself to a handful of fries. "Grow old before everything goes bad?"

"You three, yes." I picked up the newspaper and flicked through it. "I'm carrying on."

"John. You have to accept we can't alter the future." Jane began clearing the food containers away. "Why not stay here too? There's plenty of eggs."

"I always wanted to be an Inspector, you know," I said stubbornly. "I don't like mysteries. I need to see what happened for myself."

"He's a bit of a Bulldog," Florence agreed, with a tinge of regret in her voice.

"I'll don't think I *can* go any further." Jane lowered her head. "It's got to mean certain death. You can surely see that, can't you?"

I was thinking of a bold retort when my eye fell on the date on the top of the newspaper.

"Wait a minute! It's the 2nd June 1974." I scrabbled for the map in Jane's bag. "And we're only 20 miles from Akron, Ohio."

"That's where Alan Carver grew up." Florence leaned over my shoulder. "It said so in Robert Lee's newspaper article!"

"I only saw it once." Elvis thought. "Carver saved some guy being molested by a street gang, even though he was only fourteen. Became a hero."

"On the 4th ^{of} June, 1974. And it happened on Victoria Street, Akron." Florence gave me a dazzling smile. "We know exactly where he's going to be in *two* days and we're right next door."

"So we proceed one step at a time, ladies and gentlemen."

I grinned back at Florence.

"Our first move is to find the real Alan Carver and ask his opinion."

-31-

The next day we went out and bought new clothes. I was very particular about what I wanted. Black, high-necked top and a matching leather jacket.

"It's what Alan Carver was wearing when he saved that mugging victim," I explained. "Me and him better be dressed the same, otherwise people will be wondering why there are two identical teenagers walking up and down the same street. This way they'll figure they just saw the same guy twice."

We packed up and caught a Greyhound bus to Akron.

"You're the expert on Alan Carver," I said to Florence, reminded of my ignorance about his past. "What do you know about our hero's early life?"

"There's not much *to* know. Everything I could find in Robert Lee's books was either rumour or speculation." The girl wiped at the filthy window and watched cars racing down the highway. "Apparently, he had a hard childhood, but there were no real details I could find. On 4th June 1974 he saved a local businessman from a mugging and got his name in the paper. According to the article, he was on his way to a baseball match in Cleveland."

A couple of ragged kids were walking down the side of the road with their thumbs up. Florence stuck her thumb up too and got some interesting gestures back.

"And that's it. Far as anyone can tell, he disappeared that night. Didn't come to the public's attention again until he was middle-aged. Legend has it he made his fortune because he worked out a system for beating the tables at Atlantic City Casinos. The rest of his story, you already know but, by that time he was a chubby guy with a long white hair and a goatee."

She shrugged.

"Which is why nobody in New Hebrides spotted the resemblance between you and him."

"Don't remind me." I sighed. "I have no intention of ending up as a hairy fatty."

"According to the newspaper article, the mugging happened at about six in the evening." Jane popped her head over the seat. "When the bus gets to Akron, let's rent a room, buy a modern map and find Victoria Street."

We arrived early and cased the place. Victoria Street was a narrow alleyway of towering brownstones that blocked out the sun. Iron fire escapes zig zagged up to the roofs and trash cans studded the pavements. I found a length of lead pipe lying in the garbage and picked it up.

"Just like my old Baton," I grinned. "This'll do nicely."

I sent Jane and Florence up into the latticed jungle on one side of the street, while Elvis and I took the other.

Then we waited.

Ten minutes later, an overweight man in a pin-striped suit emerged from a side door, clutching his briefcase. As he made his way towards the end of the alley, a couple of shady characters silently appeared, silhouetted against the evening light. The businessman turned and hurried in the other direction.

Two more strangers appeared, cutting off his retreat.

The gang advanced on him from both sides. It was too dark in the alley to see properly but, judging by their build, they weren't much older than me. Their quarry pressed himself against the wall, choking back a sob.

"No sign of Carver." Elvis rose up from his hiding place. "Damn. We better handle this ourselves."

"I can manage." I pushed him down and waved for Florence and Jane to stay where they were too. "There's only four of them."

"Suit yourself." Elvis yawned. "I could do with a nap."

"Go ahead. This'll be a piece of cake."

I might have thought that through a bit more.

The thugs had almost reached their cowering victim. Where the hell was Alan Carver?

"Hand over the case, sucka." The largest of the gang stepped forwards.

"It's our store takings," the man pleaded. "I need this to feed my family."

"That don't make no nevermind." The youth held out his hand. "Give it here, fore I shank ya."

I couldn't wait any more. I dropped down and landed in front of the terrified man.

"Naughty, naughty." I scolded, twirling the pipe around my fingers. "This guy just wants to go home."

"We will lay the hammer *down* on you, clown." The thugs flicked their wrists and silver glinted in their hands. I remembered Florence saying they were called switchblades. I motioned for the petri-fied shopkeeper to hide and pulled out my Bowie Knife.

"Don't be put off, guys." I grinned. "It's not the size of your weapons that count. It's how you use them."

Then the banter was over and the gang attacked.

They were young and they were mean. But I was a Regulator and I had now fought cannibals, dinosaurs and cowboys. I figured that put me in a class of my own.

Blades glinted as they connected with the pipe and sparks flew in the air as we parried, kicked and punched. One assailant got in a lucky swipe, taking a nick out of my forehead, but I ignored the blood running down my face.

The louts had street smarts but no training and, within minutes, it was over. The hoodlums retreated, clutching fractured bones and broken heads.

I gave a bow to my audience above.

"Show off." Florence booed.

I didn't even see the fifth attacker. He came from the night by the wall, moving fast and low.

"Look out, John!" Jane yelled. "Behind you."

I spun and leapt back as a switchblade sliced through the air, narrowly missing my abdomen. The move brought me and my opponent into the orb of the nearest streetlight.

We both stopped dead.

Standing in front of me was Alan Carver.

"What's goin down here?" The menace in Carver's eyes turned instantly to bewilderment. "You're me! That don make no sense!"

Didn't make much sense to me either. But before I had time to reply, Carver turned and fled.

My mind was in turmoil. Alan Carver was a street thug, mugging people in alleyways! How could a guy like that possibly be the Saviour of New Hebrides?

The other Goners were equally shocked. I could hear them muttering above as I helped the shopkeeper from his hiding place.

They were about to climb down when a car drew up at the end of the alley, lights flashing. Two uniformed men leapt out and drew their guns.

"Drop the pipe, punk!" One shouted. "Lie face down on the ground."

"No, wait!" The man got in front of me. "He's innocent. He saved me from getting robbed."

Elvis and the others sank down again. Two civilians got out of the back of the car and a flashbulb went off in my face.

"We're from the Akron Gazette." A woman in a tight grey dress held up a pen and pad. "We're riding with the police, doing an article about crime on the streets."

"This boy's a genuine hero." The shopkeeper patted my arm protectively. "Fought off these armed robbers all on his own."

"Did you get a look at them?" one of the cops asked him. "Maybe pick their faces out from mug shots."

"I was hiding behind a garbage can," the man said shamefacedly.

"It was too dark for me to recognise any of them," I lied.

"What's your name, son?" the reporter asked. Her photographer took another snap.

"Hey! We know *this* perp." One of the cops took off his hat and scratched his head. "Name's Alan Carver. He's only fifteen and already got a rap sheet as long as the Hope Bridge. Boosting cars. Burglary. Assault. You name it."

"He knows how to tangle, all right," the other officer reluctantly put away his gun. "I never seen him *help* anyone before."

"Everyone deserves a second chance," I said lamely.

"I got nearly two thousand dollars in this bag and I'd have been ruined if those hooligans had got it." The businessman fished in his pocket and pressed two paper squares into my hand. "Here's a couple of tickets for the Rangers/Indian game in Cleveland tonight as a reward. Best seats in the house. It doesn't start for a couple of hours, so you can catch it if you grab a bus now."

"I appreciate it." I had no use for the tickets but it seemed rude to turn them down. "If the officers don't object, I'll do just that."

"Go on, get out of here." The Lawman gave me a whack on the head. "If we didn't have these hacks with us you'd be straight downtown in the back of a meat wagon."

I wasn't sure why police would be hauling beef around but I let it slide.

"You're all heart." I turned and trotted away. I could meet the others back at the hotel once the excitement had died down.

"Get the *Akron Gazette* tomorrow," the reporter shouted after me. "Your picture will be in it and we'd like to do a follow-up story."

I made my way through the darkened streets. This part of Akron looked even rougher than Cleveland, but I didn't pay much attention to my surroundings. Instead, I stopped and stared at myself in a darkened shop window. I was much thinner than I'd been in New Hebrides and my hair had grown. I was wearing a black top and jacket and I had a fresh Goner down my face from the fight.

Alan Carver existed all right. But *he* wasn't the boy in the precious newspaper clipping Robert Ropemaker Lee had shown me on the island.

The person in that picture was *me*.

I felt something sharp press against my neck and a figure stepped out of the shadowy doorway to my right.

"You and me got a score to settle, turkey. You dig?"

It was the real Alan Carver.

"I bet you have a few questions first." I slowly held my arms away from my body. "The main one bein why I look exactly like you."

"Only reason you ain't lying in a pool of your own blood."

I kicked backwards, catching Carver's knee. As he tilted sideways, I ducked away from the knife and elbowed him in the chest. The boy landed on his back and swept a leg round, knocking me off my feet. Then he was on top of me, switchblade raised. I chopped it away and he butted me in the face. I grabbed his ears and twisted. Carver jerked away with a howl and slammed his palm into my throat. I threw him off and scrabbled away as he retrieved his blade.

We faced each other on our hands and knees, teeth bared.

"We could do this all night," I wheezed. "Or we could go grab a Coke and talk. I get the feeling we're both looking for answers, and we won't get them kicking seven bells out of each other."

Carver glared at me suspiciously.

"All right, chump," he said finally. "We can have a confab. But I want a cheeseburger as well as the skinny, and you're frontin the moolah."

I agreed, though I didn't have a clue what he'd actually said.

We found an all-night diner on the corner. As Alan entered, I glanced back and spotted Elvis, Florence and Jane following at a respectful pace. I motioned for them to stay where they were.

We got ourselves a booth at the window and, for a while, just stared at each other. It was like looking in a mirror at my evil twin.

"I can't believe I got a brother and mamma never told me." Carver took a bite of his burger. "You musta been adopted when we were babies."

"I'm not your brother."

"Don't yank my chain, buddy. Take a good look atcha self."

"I'm you, Alan."

"What the hell does that mean?"

This was going to be harder than I thought. One thing was certain, this guy was no genius. So what did I say next?

Actually, I'm from the future but I'm also from the past. And we need you to save the world when you're finished being Public Enemy Number One.

That wouldn't wash. If I was Alan Carver, I'd stab me right there and be done with it. But I *was* Alan Carver and I knew this about myself.

I was a curious type.

"I have some people with me," I began. "Waiting outside…"

Carver's hand immediately went to the pocket where he kept his switchblade.

"And, if we were going to ambush you, I wouldn't have *mentioned* them."

God, he was a suspicious sort.

The hand stayed where it was. I slowly took the Bowie Knife from inside my jacket, placed it on the table and pushed it towards him.

"I'd like to invite them in. If they try anything violent in a brightly lit diner full of witnesses, feel free to use this."

"I hear ya." Carver slid my knife onto his lap. "Choice shiv, by the way."

I beckoned at the dark window, knowing my friends were out there watching. Seconds later, the others joined us at the table and ordered Cokes and fries. The sight of Florence and Jane cheered Carver up no end.

"Foxy bunnies, operator. Respect!" He leered at Jane, who sniffed disdainfully.

"No need to give me the hairy eyeball, baby."

"This is Jane Austen, Florence Nightingale and Elvis Presley."

"Sit on it, cats. What's your real names?"

Elvis looked puzzled. "These *are* our names."

"I'm down with that." Carver nodded. "Best to have a fake handle so the fuzz ain't got jack when they scope you out."

"I got no idea what he just told me," Elvis complained.

"Florence." I threw up my hands. "What do I say to him?"

"Yeah, hot pants." Carver leaned his chin on one hand and winked at her. "What's shakin here?"

Florence glanced around and spotted a TV above the counter. A bunch of guys in stripy outfits were running around waving bats.

"You follow baseball, Alan?"

"Sure." He pointed to the screen. "Game's just started. Cleveland Indians versus the Texas Rangers." He chuckled. "Tubular! They're giving out cups of beer for 10 cents each to the fans. Once in a lifetime offer, you dig?"

"Oh, it *will* be." Florence closed her eyes and I could almost hear that photographic memory clicking into action. "Early in the game, the Rangers take a 5-1 lead."

"Jump back, sister. We gonna whump those suckas."

"An inebriated woman will run towards the Indian's on-deck circle soon and flash her boobs."

"For real?" Carver's eyes lit up. "Hold on a minute…"

"Then a naked man streaks across the pitch and a father and son follow and moon the audience."

"I heard enough of this static." Carver made to stand. "I'm splittin."

"God, it's hardly started and the Indians are down 5-1," the guy behind the counter groaned.

Carver sat down again, eyes glued to the TV.

"Cleveland's Leron Lee hits a line drive into the stomach of Ranger's pitcher Ferguson Jenkins." Florence was on a roll. "The Rangers manager gets pelted with hot dogs, then there's a full scale riot. The Indians join with the Rangers and begin hitting the fans with baseball bats."

A woman darted onto the field and pulled up her top. Carver's mouth dropped open.

"Cleveland eventually forfeit the game with the score tied 5-5 in the ninth." Florence sat back and did a drum roll on the table.

"That's the perils of alcohol for you."

Carver watched the rest of the game, transfixed. The transmission was eventually shut down when the match descended into a pitched battle between players and spectators armed with torn up stadium seats.

"That game on the boob tube?" Alan Carver asked the waitress in a small voice. "Was it live?"

"Naw. We have little people in the TV acting out scenarios." The woman curled her lip. "Of course it's live. You kids gonna buy anything else or sit eating cold fries all night?"

"Who *are* you freaky cats?" Carver shrank away from us. "I'm out to lunch on this scene."

"Come back to our hotel room." I waved for the cheque. "We have a *lot* to talk about."

"As long as you can manage actual English." Jane leaned over and pinched Carver's cheek.

"*Cat.*"

<h1 style="text-align:center">-32-</h1>

"Got any smokes in this fooey pad?" Alan Carver plonked himself on one of the tatty beds and looked disdainfully around our cramped room. "No? You rah rah's are *so* square."

"Why would you mug someone, Alan?" Florence couldn't keep the disappointment from her voice. "You almost took the poor guy's life savings."

"Up your nose with a rubber hose." Carver's hand instinctively went to the pocket where he kept his switchblade. "That's how you survive in the hood."

"Don't you go to school?" The girl sat down next to him. "What about your mum and dad?"

"I never knew my pop." The boy gave a bitter bark of laughter. "An my mom drank herself to death a couple of years ago. I been to reform school, but all the man taught you there was how to get reamed, catch my drift? So I ran away."

He glowered at me.

"I saw them reporters take a picture of you, by the way."

"They're going to put it in the paper tomorrow," I admitted.

"That's *my* street cred shot to hell." He put his head in his hands. "The local bloods are gonna think it was *me* saving that cat, an getting brotherly with the pigs, to boot. What a nightmare. I may as well blow town right now."

"Have you got a guy who receives stolen goods for you?" Elvis asked.

"You mean a fence?" Carver's eyes narrowed. "Why do you wanna know?"

"Could he fence this?" Elvis tossed the boy a canvas bag. Carver opened it and almost fell off the bed when he saw the gold dust.

"This is *serious* bread," he gawped, sifting his fingers through the yellow grains. "You guys hold up a bank?"

"Actually, we did."

"Get straight!" The boy couldn't take his eyes off the fortune on his lap. "Banks don't carry gold dust."

"They did in 1876." Elvis took the bag back and stashed it in the wardrobe. "That's when we robbed it."

"We're time travellers," I added unnecessarily.

The *cat* was well and truly out of the bag now. And halfway up a tree.

Alan Carver looked at us for a long time. Then he began to laugh. He slapped one thigh, throwing back his head and guffawing until his shoulders shook.

"That's wack." He wiped tears from his eyes. "You must think I'm some kinda doofus."

"It doesn't matter if you believe us," I snapped. "The gold is yours if you do what we ask."

The laughter stopped instantly.

"Who do you want me to kill?" he said. "You're looking for a hitman, aintcha?"

"Can you take a walk?" I realized I *really* didn't like Alan Carver. "I need a little time to talk to my friends."

"What's to stop me coming back with some homies and relieving you cheese weasels of your inky stash?"

"Apart from the fact that most of them have broken bones?" Jane raised an eyebrow. "Look under the bed."

Carver did. It was where we'd hidden our weapons.

"Unreal! You're packing enough hardware to break into Fort Knox." His muffled voice floated up. "I guess I'll come back on my own and get the low-down, after all." He sat up and blew air through pursed lips. "Got to say, I'm plenty curious now."

I *knew* it.

Once he was gone, I sank back on the bed with an exhausted sigh.

"I don't get this. There's *no* way that moron is the founder of New Hebrides."

"But he is," Florence objected. "We know he is."

"He's a self-serving, violent cretin." I clenched my fists. "But what hurts most is that he's me!" I looked around for reassurance. "He's not really *like* me, guys. *Is* he?"

Elvis moved to the widow, hands behind his back. Florence stared at the ceiling.

"Yeah… you were a bit like that to begin with." It was left to Jane to be brutally honest. "We all hated you, remember?"

"I didn't." Florence corrected. "Anyhow, you've changed. You've been willing to make sacrifices for your cause and for your friends."

"That's because I thought I was the carbon copy of a great man and an inspirational leader. The thug we just met isn't any of those so, obviously, neither am I."

There. I'd said it.

"We followed *you*, not Alan Carver." Jane shot back. "And we made the right choice, because you got us this far. Maybe Carver will shape up too."

But she didn't sound convinced and neither were the rest of us.

Ever since I was a baby, I'd been taught to uphold the law. It was ingrained in me to serve and protect, no matter how misguided that instinct. Alan Carver, on the other hand, had been raised a lawbreaker and an opportunist. If we gave him our fortune in gold, he wouldn't use it to better himself or help the rest of the world. He'd vanish and spend it on himself.

"I need some air."

I stumbled out onto the fire escape and leaned on the rail, taking deep breaths, inhaling the scent of petrol fumes and late night cooking. In the distance, car horns sobbed and I could hear a couple in the tenement opposite arguing behind drawn curtains. Once again, my determination to be someone had led to failure. Like Alan Carver, I was nothing but a cheap hood, trying to make a big score.

Florence emerged from the room and stood beside me. She picked at a stray hair the wind had blown into her mouth.

"You're not giving up, are you?" she asked.

"I've already said I'll keep going, for all the good it will do." I fingered the Goner on my forehead. "But I still want the rest of you to stay here, sell the gold and build decent lives for yourselves."

"Listen carefully to what I have to say." Florence took my hand. "The world needs an Alan

Carver to save it, sure. But it needs the *right* one at the right time."

"I don't understand."

"It took a tough, driven, resourceful Alan Carver to get us to this point - and you were perfect for that. Now it needs another sort of Alan Carver to take over." She smiled grimly. "And you're right. It's not the light fingered yahoo we just met. He's probably off jacking a car as we speak."

She laughed softly to herself.

"He *is* cute, though."

"Not as cute as me, I hope."

"No. You've got a sexy scar." She examined it. "It'll heal, though, and you two will be identical again."

Suddenly it dawned on me just what Florence was talking about.

"Are you saying I should become Alan Carver in this *time* period?" My mind reeled at the thought. "Get rid of the useless one and take his place?"

To my surprise, she shook her head.

"Your DNA had to have come from the original Alan Carver. You *can't* be a replica of yourself, because time travel doesn't work that way." She squeezed my hand tighter. "I love you, but you aren't the saviour of New Hebrides."

"You love me?" I felt my heart leap.

"Not the time, John."

"Well… it can't be that moron, either. He could never have invented all that amazing stuff we had on the island."

"No, he couldn't." Florence let go of my hand and turned away, leaning her elbows on the cold railing. "As far as I can see, there's only one person up to that job."

And suddenly, I got it. The photographic memory. The ability to mentally calculate huge numbers. The brains to come up with a time travel formula that predicted which dates we'd encounter, all without any kind of schooling.

"You're talking about *yourself*."

"This is *my* most precious possession." The girl removed a locket from around her neck, fiddled with the clasp and opened it. "Robert Lee gave it to me."

She unfolded the bit of paper inside and handed it over.

It was a picture torn from a book. It showed a long haired, chunky middle-aged male standing with a group of people in white coats. I recognised him as the adult Alan Carver from the statues I used to see dotted around New Hebrides.

"Look at the woman on the far left." Florence closed her eyes. "The one trying desperately to leave before her photograph was taken."

She had short white hair and lines creased her forehead and eyes. It took a few seconds for recognition to sink in, but there was no mistaking the face.

"That's *you*!"

"Carver wants to be rich and, somehow, he'll have the street smarts to turn our gold into a fortune." Florence tilted her head back and looked up at the stars. "I'll need his wealth to found New Hebrides and the Carver Foundation in his name."

My head was spinning.

"You *knew* it was going to come to this." I gave her back the picture. "You knew it all along."

A gust of cold air blew across the fire escape but I didn't feel it.

"I'm so sorry." She opened her fingers and let the page drift away on the night breeze. "I hoped with all my heart something else would work out. But it didn't."

She grabbed my arm.

"Don't let my life be a waste, John Wayne," she begged. "If I stay here, you have to take Elvis and Jane into the future and try to save our home. *Promise* me."

"But I can't!" Tears welled up in my eyes. "We can't change anything."

"*Promise* me you'll try."

"I'll try." I straightened my shoulders. "I give you my word."

"You're a good man." She rubbed her bare arms. "I never doubted it."

Moonlight shone in her ebony hair and the neon from the streetlight sparkled in her eyes. She was smarter and better than the rest of us put together and I had never appreciated it.

"Florence." I reached out. "I need to tell you how I feel…"

"Don't you *dare* say it." She moved quickly away. "This is hard enough."

There was a knock on the window.

"Your better half is here, John." Elvis stuck his head out. "Says he's brought Jack Daniels, whoever that is."

"Be right in."

Once Elvis had retreated, the girl turned to me.

"Stop trying to be Alan Carver and start being *you*." She put her hands sternly on both hips. She'd obviously learned a thing or two from Jane. "Cause, from now on, I'll be trying to turn Alan Carver into John Wayne."

"Who the hell *is* John Wayne anyway?" It was a rhetorical question but Florence answered it.

"He was an actor. Played the tough guy who always knew right from wrong."

She kissed me on the lips.

"And he beat the odds, no matter what it took."

"Don't fake me out, cats. Why you figuring to fork over gobs of money and what do I have to do to get it?" Alan Carver plonked himself in a chair and poured himself a glass of nasty-smelling liquid. "Want a drink?"

"No thanks." Elvis wrinkled his nose in disgust. "I already tried coffee."

"We have four bags of gold dust." I opened the wardrobe to reveal our bounty. "We're giving it all to you, though I'm not sure what it's worth."

"Wowzers." Carver eyed the bags hungrily. "That would fetch primo dollars."

"The deal is… you take the gold and vanish." I said. "Get yourself straightened out and start using the money to make an even bigger fortune. I don't care how you do it."

"I can get behind that." The boy held up his glass. "But, like I said, what's the catch?"

"Me." Florence stood over him. "You take me with you."

Elvis and Jane glanced at each other.

"Zoinks! I ain't no babysitter, even for a foxy mama." Carver spluttered. "I'm a free spirit, dig?"

"I'm not finished." Florence put hands on her hips again. "Once you've made enough, you'll put me through college so I can get a science degree. Get me a fake ID and qualifications, if you have to. I'm sure you'll be capable of it, given your past."

"What if I just peel out on the deal?"

"We'll find you, like we did before." Jane crouched between his legs and looked straight into his eyes. "Then I'll kill you. Painfully."

"I'd take that threat *very* seriously," Elvis muttered.

"Chill, man." Carver coolly took another sip of his drink. "I'm down with that. It ain't no thing."

"The deal is sealed." Florence removed the glass from his hand. "We'll meet you at the bus station tomorrow with the gold. It's your choice where you and I go."

"I always had good vibes about Atlantic City," Carver pursed his lips. "It's got a lot of Casinos." He looked Florence up and down. "Oughtta be gravy, hanging with a cute babe like you."

"Especially one who can work out a formula to beat the gambling tables."

"You're able do that?" the boy sputtered.

"Shouldn't be a problem."

"Far out!" Carver blew her a kiss as he headed for the door. "You is suddenly my dream girl!"

As soon as he was gone, Jane and Elvis rounded on Florence.

"You're *staying* with that jerk?"

"If I don't, he'll blow any money we give him in a heartbeat." The girl grabbed a pen and began to write equations on it. "At least I'll be safe."

She finished her calculations with a flourish.

"But I don't know about you. Like I predicted, the next barrier will take whoever crosses it into the heart of the Great Chaos."

"Can you be specific about the date?" I asked.

"I can't pin it down exactly, but my best guess is August 2019."

"That's the month and year that Alan Carver was killed," Jane said. "He never made it to the waiting helicopter."

"I wouldn't mention *that* to him. He's unreliable enough."

"Florence, how come we keep arriving at pivotal moments in history?" Elvis counted off events on his fingers. "Man discovering fire. Custer's Last Stand. Alan Carver's aborted mugging."

"We're not *arriving* at them." I snapped my fingers as the truth dawned on me. "We're *causing* them!"

"You got it." The girl patted my arm. "Now, ask yourself this. In the future, why didn't Alan Carver escape to New Hebrides and save himself when he had the chance? You saw what he's like."

"He was waiting for *us*?"

"Why not? What if he found something he *had* to tell you?" Florence nodded. "Something so important it was worth sacrificing his life for?"

"Looks like me and Jane will be tagging along after all, John." Elvis fished a colt from under the bed and stuffed it in his bag. "I always was a curious type."

Touché.

Florence picked up the discarded bottle of Jack Daniels.

"Let's have a drink to absent friends." She poured a hefty measure into her chipped cup. "I'll be one of them tomorrow."

So we laughed and talked into the small hours. But none of us mentioned the future again.

It was too painful.

Next morning we met Alan Carver and caught the bus to Atlantic City. Just before we reached the town centre, Elvis spotted a glittering curtain stretching across a run-down parking lot to the east.

"Just let us off here," I told the driver.

"We're only ten minutes from the station," Carver objected.

"I know." Jane escorted him, protesting, from the bus. "But you're going to want to see this."

"When we've made enough money, we'll build the Carver Foundation labs right here," Florence said to me. "Once you go through the barrier, turn round and you'll be looking right at them."

"What labs? What Foundation?" Carver screwed up his face. "What *barrier*?"

"It's one you can't see and your new companion refuses to cross." Jane pulled the boy to one side. "Just watch."

"I'll be back in 46 years." I pulled Florence close and kissed her cheek. "Though that seems a really weird thing to say."

"I'll be waiting."

"I wish it could have turned out differently." Elvis wrapped her in a bear hug. "I really do."

"Me too."

Jane hung back. Then, for the first and last time, I saw her cry.

"I love you, girl." Her face crumpled. "You're my best friend."

Florence pulled her close and held her tight.

"I don't get it." Alan Carver stuck both hands into his pockets and turned to me. "You ain't going to the moon. Hell, you couldn't even make it to the bus station."

Jane and Elvis waved and vanished through the barrier that Carver obviously couldn't see.

"Shut up!" The boy went white. "Where did they *go*?"

He turned to me, biting his lip.

"All that time travel stuff. It's… for *real*?"

"It is." I put a hand on his shoulder. "Which is how we know the survival of the human race depends on *you*."

"That's a heavy trip, man. Sure you got the right guy?"

I turned him in the direction of Florence.

"It also depends on *her*. The best thing that ever happened to either of us."

"Then I'll treat her right." Alan Carver looked me in the eye. "You go do your freaky thang."

"Thank you."

"One question." As I turned to go, he pulled me back. "If you got the low down on the future, can you say what happens to yours truly?"

"I honestly don't know," I lied.

"Don't ask, don't tell, huh?" To my surprise, he reached out and shook my hand. "Keep on trucking, man. I owe you."

He turned his back so I could bid goodbye to Florence. But there wasn't much I could say. My throat was too constricted.

"Bye Mower." I kissed her forehead. "I mean… *Scientist*."

"So long, Regulator. When we meet again, please don't mention the grey hairs."

I gently touched her cheek. Then I turned away and stepped through the barrier.

Part 5

When I was a child, I spoke as a child, I felt as a child, I thought as a child. Now that I have become a man, I have put away childish things.

1 Corinthians 13:11

<h1 style="text-align:center">-33-</h1>

The parking lot was gone. Instead, we found ourselves in a square compound next to a bunch of armoured jeeps. The perimeter was ringed by two security fences, topped with vicious strands of barbed wire and patrolled by guards dressed in the green uniform of the New Hebrides Militia. Pressed against the barrier was a large mob of people, faces pale and fearful, stretching pleading hands through the mesh.

Beyond that, Atlantic City was burning, a pall of black smoke hanging over ruined buildings. It was a lot to take in at one glance.

I turned round. Behind me was a box shaped building with the legend Carver Foundation emblazoned across the front in yellow neon.

"Appropriate for a town filled with Casinos," Jane snorted. "Alan Carver certainly hasn't lost touch with his roots."

A patrol emerged from the building and ran towards us. They too wore the uniforms of Carver's armed forces.

"Are you the Goners?" A man with Lieutenant's insignia stopped and saluted. "We've been expecting you."

"Were you expecting us to appear out of thin air?" Elvis commented dryly. "You seem awfully calm about it."

"As a matter of fact, I can't believe my eyes." The Lieutenant replied stoically. "But Alan Carver said it would happen and he's never wrong."

He turned and marched towards the building.

"I'll show you to your quarters so you can freshen up." He indicated for us to follow. "Then Mr Carver will see you."

We were led up several flights of stairs to an immaculate white suite. On the table was a bowl of fruit and a tray of sandwiches. Draped over the back of a leather couch were towels, bathrobes and three crimson uniforms.

We found an adjoining bathroom and took turns getting cleaned up. Jane went last, emerging from the bathroom to find Elvis and I fully dressed and tucking into snacks.

"That's just great." She stood with hands on her hips. "You're Regulators again."

"Red looks good on *you*, though," Elvis whistled at the tight top. "Brings out the hatred in your eyes."

"Look," I said happily. "I can fit the colt in my Baton holster."

"I can't work out what you love most," Jane grunted. "Yourself or that damned gun."

"It's a dead heat."

There was a tap on the door and a bald man stuck his head round.

"Are you decent?"

"Yup."

The stranger stepped inside. He wore blue jeans and a white shirt with the sleeves rolled up.

"Don't you *recognise* me?"

Our expressions obviously indicated we didn't.

"I'm Alan Carver!"

I looked at him carefully. It took a while but, eventually, I realised it really was him. However, he no longer bore any resemblance to the statues I had seen in New Hebrides.

Carver was fit and muscular and, despite crow's feet round his eyes, he certainly didn't look his sixty years. I had to admit, I was pretty relieved about that.

"Where's the long hair?" I goggled. "The goatee?"

"Shaved it all off." He patted his head self-consciously. "We don't have time for personal grooming in this place."

"But you're thin!"

"Tell me about it. The food here is rationed and I've lost about 40 pounds." He strode over and shook my hand. "Delighted to see you again, John. Elvis? Jane?" He gave each a short embrace. "Welcome back. I hope the sandwiches were satisfactory. Everybody likes cheese."

"Glad to see you learned proper English," Jane said through a mouthful of crumbs. "Now I can understand you without a translator."

"I'm not a teenage tearaway anymore," Carver smirked. "But I can totally remember that gig if you're jonesin on it, catch my drift?"

"Please don't."

"Where's Florence Nightingale?" Elvis peered over his shoulder. "Is she ok?"

"Florence Nightingale!" Carver laughed out loud. "She hasn't been called *that* in a long time." He kicked open the door with his foot. "But I *would* like to present to you the love of my life. Mrs F N Carver."

And there she was. Florence's hair had thick grey streaks and her forehead was criss-crossed with worry lines. But she still looked beautiful.

"I got old," she said shyly, hanging back.

I tried to make a joke but, for once, nothing came out. Instead, I threw myself forwards and squeezed her so hard that her breath escaped in an unladylike grunt. We surrounded her, laughing and crying as she tried to hug us all at once.

"You got the same figure as when we left," Jane said enviously.

"Not a lot of provisions left and I took up swimming as a hobby." Florence winked at her husband. "In Atlantic City, there's nothing else to do but gamble, and my better half already had *that* covered."

Alan Carver stood back, beaming.

"We can catch up later." Florence finally managed to shove us away, though she was still smiling. "But we're kind of pressed for time. I'm sure you saw the mob outside the compound gates."

"The Great Chaos?"

"Doesn't even begin to describe it." She was suddenly solemn. "There's no food or water to be had out there but we have jeeps and supplies. They're desperate to get in and I don't blame them."

"Sit yourself down." Alan took a chair while we made room on the huge couch for Florence. "I'll give you a quick appraisal of the situation."

"Have you found a cure for the Golden Plague?" I saw no point in beating around the bush.

"No, we haven't." Seeing our crestfallen faces, Carver leaned forwards earnestly. "But Florence has made big inroads recently. I reckon she *could* do it, if we only had enough time."

"How long are you talking about?"

"A year. Maybe even eight months." Florence took up the thread. "But we don't have nearly that long. The crowds are bigger and bolder every day and there's a rumour armed military deserters are heading this way."

I leaned back and gave a frustrated moan. I'd failed.

"It's not as bad as it seems." Carver patted my knee. "The US and Canadian governments have established research labs in Newfoundland. It's so remote up there that the wheat is still months away."

He looked at his watch.

"Florence insisted we stay until you arrived." He smiled again. "We wanted to give you the chance to come along."

Elvis and Jane exchanged glances.

"Sounds like a plan," I said. "You think we could have a few minutes alone with her, though? She hasn't seen us in forty years."

"Of course." Carver stood and kissed his wife tenderly. "I'll be in the labs, honey."

"Ok. Don't stay up too late."

"You didn't tell him, did you?" Once our host was gone, I stood up and paced the room. "You didn't *tell* him what happens."

"Carver never found a cure for the Golden Plague," Jane joined in. "Not in Newfoundland or anywhere else."

"I know that!" Florence's lip trembled. "What was I supposed to do? Blithely inform the man I love that his entire life's work – a career I *pushed* him into – was doomed to come to nothing."

I could see her point.

"Couldn't you both just leave for New Hebrides?" I suggested. "At least you could save yourselves."

"He won't go." The woman shook her head vehemently. "Do you know why?"

"Eh, no. We just got here."

"Because there's one more barrier between Atlantic City and the island." Florence gritted her teeth. "If we both tried to get there, he'd end up in the New Hebrides of 2016. But I'd go through the time rift and arrive 150 years later."

"Ah."

"He wouldn't hear of being separated from me and I will *not* leave that wonderful man." She patted her eyes with a napkin. "We're going to Newfoundland to spend what time we have left together."

"I can dig that, cat."

The others glared at me.

"Sorry. Couldn't help myself."

"You have a helicopter on the roof." Jane was as straightforward as ever. "That what you intend to take?"

"Of course not. It was sent by New Hebrides to take us back, but we're not going. We'll put the last DNA samples on it instead."

Florence pointed out of the window.

"Instead, we'll use those armoured jeeps to lead a convoy north. It'll be dangerous, but we're heavily armed. Problem is, we have to open the gates to get out and that will let the mob in. It's why we had to wait for you."

"Count me in." Jane reached into her bag and pulled out a revolver. "I'm sure you could use three extra guns."

"Florence." Elvis looked at the ground. "I'm sorry, but we all know our history. Doesn't Alan Carver die trying to reach that helicopter?"

"The records could be wrong and my husband is an exceptional man!" The woman rounded on him angrily. "He'll figure out a way to get around the problem. I just know it."

I didn't see how that was remotely possible and, judging by my companions' expressions, neither did they. But what could we say?

"I tried so hard." Florence began to cry. "We went right round the world! I spent my life working on a cure! How could all that effort have come to nothing?"

"We all did our best." Jane pulled the woman close and kissed her cheek. "At least now, we'll be together."

I sat back and watched the Goners console each other. Sure, we could go to Newfoundland and live out the rest of our lives with each other. In a way, that would be a fine thing. But it wasn't saving the world.

It wasn't good enough.

I found Alan Carver in his lab, helping three white-coated scientists load plastic discs into a metal container.

"The last of the DNA samples to go to New Hebrides," he explained, holding up a sheet of paper. "It's everybody in the building. We haven't had time to catalogue them properly, but the names and occupations are on this."

"Is your DNA in there?"

"Sample 27."

"That's very modest," I said admiringly. "I'd have made myself number 1."

"I got my reasons. Want a soda?"

"Yes please."

Alan fetched one, then sat down at his desk.

"I've done everything that Florence asked me, John." He poured a glass of wine from the crystal decanter by his elbow. "I figure I'm owed the truth from *somebody*."

"Can't argue with that."

"My wife wants me to be happy and I can dig that. So she's always insisted that I survive and her efforts lead to a cure for the Golden Plague."

He took a slow sip and looked at me over the rim of the glass.

"That's not true, is it?"

I hesitated for a long time. But Alan Carver was me and I'd done enough lying to myself.

"I'm from your island, a century and a half from now." I opened the can and set it down. "We're all that's left of the human race and, no, we still haven't found a cure."

"What about me?"

"According to the helicopter pilot, the mob breaks in and you're killed trying to reach his chopper."

"Thanks for being honest." Alan opened a drawer and pulled out a lighter. He held it under the list of names until the paper caught fire.

"What are you up to, Alan?"

"If the folks at New Hebrides had a labelled and confirmed sample of my DNA, what would they do with it?"

"They'd reincarnate it straight away and put you in charge of the project."

"Of course they would." Carver watched the last shreds of paper curl into ash. "Which would be a disaster. Florence is the genius, even though I took all the glory."

He gave a heartfelt sigh.

"I'm a hustler and a great money maker, but I'm no scientist."

"Preaching to the converted. But, for what it's worth, I think you would have made a fine leader."

"I don't want the responsibility." He drained his glass and poured another. "We're about to make a horrific decision, you and I. After that, I just want to live a quiet life. What's more important, I want to live my *own* life, without destiny dictating my every move."

"You're not listening, Alan." Now I understood why Florence had lied. But I couldn't do that. I just couldn't. "You don't *make* it out of here. The past is fixed and it can't be changed."

"Oh, I intend to survive, all right." He gave a bark of bitter laughter. "But it will be at a terrible price."

"Yeah… You did mention a horrific decision," I said cautiously. "One that *we* were going to make?"

"I'm sorry to lay this on you, kid." Alan Carver poured a second glass and handed it to me. This time I accepted.

"Here's what we have to do and nobody else can know about it…"

When our conversation was over, I went back to the Goners' quarters. Elvis and Jane were sitting on the couch. They moved apart quickly as I entered.

"Where have you been?" Elvis looked flushed. "We were just.. eh… talking."

"Having my first ever glass of wine."

"Come sit with us." Jane patted the seat. "It didn't work out as we'd hoped, but we gave it a damned good go."

"I'm going to turn in." I shook my head. "Leave you guys alone."

"You sure?"

"I'm sure." I turned to go, then halted. "You both need to stay alive, however bleak things get, you hear?"

"I was planning on doing just that," Elvis said bravely.

"Good." I grabbed the last sandwich on the plate. "Have faith in me, no matter what happens. I'm begging you."

"Sure." They looked puzzled. "You got it, boss."

I went to bed and spent the night thinking about what Carver had proposed and staring into the darkness.

<h1 style="text-align:center">-34-</h1>

I was woken by the sound of firearms. Jane burst into my room, fully dressed and strapping on her gun.

"Up now." She threw me my clothes. "The mob have broken in."

I pulled on my uniform and ran into the living room. Elvis was leaning out of the window.

"We're in big trouble."

The crowd had pushed down the fence by sheer weight of numbers and were surging across the compound. Some wore the uniforms of US troops and carried rifles. The guards had managed to get the jeeps into a circle and were returning fire, while more New Hebrides forces streamed from the Foundation.

Some made it to the vehicles. Others were shot down or pulled to pieces by the crowd, who then snatched up the fallen weapons and turned them on the defenders. The mob surged towards the front door of the building, their front ranks falling under a withering hail of fire. But they pressed on.

"This is bad." Jane appeared at my shoulder.

"You're a master of understatement." I unholstered my colt. "You and Elvis get down there now. Those vehicles won't wait much longer."

"We'll never make it."

"I'll cover you from the roof. I spotted a mounted cannon up there yesterday." I raised an eyebrow. "Let's hope this one points down."

"We're not *leaving* you."

"Remember what I said last night?" I grabbed Elvis and pulled him away from the window. "I have a plan. *Get going*!"

"All right." The boy squared up to me. "But if you're lying and you die, I'll come back and dig you up. Then I'll kill you again myself."

"Comforting."

"You're a crazy guy." Jane kissed me full on the lips. "But I love you for what you're doing."

"I'm definitely not dying now."

We raced out of the apartment. Jane and Elvis fled down the stairs and I went up.

There was nobody on the roof except the pilot, waiting anxiously in the chopper. I sprinted to the mounted gun and swung it down. I didn't want to shoot into the crowd, for there were women down there. But it was us or them and the future of humanity was at stake.

I guess history does repeat itself.

I switched the cannon to automatic and opened fire.

Huge gaps opened in the ranks of the attackers, as bullets raked their forces, tearing up the earth in great gobs. Seizing their chance, the last defenders of the Carver Foundation emerged from the building and fought their way towards the jeeps. I could see Elvis and Jane in the middle, blasting while they ran.

I covered them as best I could until they reached the vehicles and flung themselves inside. The circle of steel roared into life as the convoy uncoiled and headed through the ruined gates. Behind me the helicopter gave a low whine and its blades began to rotate.

Florence Nightingale appeared on the roof, hair dishevelled.

"I can't find Alan!" she wailed, sprinting to the parapet and peering over. The convoy was already halfway down the street and vanishing in the distance.

"Stop!" she screamed. "Come back, you cowards!"

"Get in the chopper." I hauled her away from the edge.

"No! It can't happen like this!"

"I will *not* let your husband die!" I shoved her towards the bird. "You have to trust me! But I can't save him if I'm looking out for you."

With a strangled sob, Florence climbed aboard. I pulled out my colt and knelt down.

A man in a white shirt and blue jeans emerged from the stairwell at the other end of the building, closely followed by the baying mob. I fired again and again at the crowd.

It was no use. A shot ran out and the figure collapsed. The mob trampled him underfoot, heading for the helicopter. I struggled to my feet as it began to rise, running towards it and throwing myself into the cockpit.

Seconds later, the chopper was in the air and heading over the city. Below us, I could see the convoy fighting its way north.

"You promised me!" Florence wept. "You gave me your word!"

"I'm not dead, honey." The pilot glanced backwards at her. "How much trouble would I be in if I let *that* happen?"

It was Alan Carver.

"What? *How?*" Florence grabbed her husband and covered him in kisses.

"Stop that, woman." He fended her off with one hand. "I'll crash the damned ride."

"Who was the guy in the white shirt?"

"His name was Zac Rutter. The real pilot." Alan turned back and concentrated on the controls. "We swapped outfits. He's a hero and the most decent guy I ever met."

He pushed the throttle forward.

"Looked a lot like an older version of Elvis."

I felt a numbness spread through me. Now I know who my friend's DNA had come from.

"Wait? Where are you going, baby?" Florence looked down. "This isn't the way to Newfoundland. We're over the ocean."

I gritted my teeth. Then I reached over and squeezed her neck.

Florence's eyes rolled up in her head as she passed out.

I put on my life preserver and manoeuvred the unconscious woman into hers. Then I sat with her head on my lap while Alan headed for New Hebrides.

"When I was a little kid, I was actually a pretty decent guy." Carver didn't turn round. "It was a tough neighbourhood and all the other children ran wild. Me? I liked to read books. Dinosaur stuff mainly."

"You'd have loved where I've been," I said blankly. "I see plenty of them."

"Oh, I would," he chuckled. "When the other kids were learning how to use knives, I just wanted to shoot cans in the backyard with my catapult. Pretended they were Raptors and Tyrannosuars. But then my mum died and I turned to crime to scrape a living."

I swallowed hard.

"When did you learn to fly?"

"As soon as I had enough money," he grinned. "Always dreamed of being a pilot. Free as a bird and able to go where I pleased. Just didn't turn out that way."

I reached into my pocket and pulled out the wooden catapult I'd found in the deserted plane, back in the Cretaceous era.

"Take this," I said. "It saved my life once."

"Cool beans." Carver stuck it into the bag beside him. "It's just like the one I had."

"We're almost there," I said softly. "I can see the time barrier."

"I'll slow down and go low." Carver still didn't turn around. "You grab Florence and jump. The water will wake her up."

"Don't you want to say goodbye?"

"More than life itself. But if I look into her eyes, I'll change my mind."

"She'll hate you for this, Alan."

"Not just me, John." He finally turned round.

"F N and I couldn't have kids, but I don't regret that." He reached out and shook my hand. "If I did have a son? I'd hope he'd have turned out like you."

He swooped down.

"Bye, kid."

"Fly safe, Alan."

I pulled Florence into my arms and jumped.

She revived as soon as we hit the water.

I expected hysterics. Screaming and shouting.

But she simply watched the helicopter as it headed for New Hebrides and a different time period. I wanted to sink below the waves and drown, but the life preserver kept me afloat.

"Florence…" I began.

"Shut up." She stared at the chopper until it was only a speck.

"This was the only way to save the human race." I tried again. "You have the knowledge and New Hebrides has the recourses."

"So does Newfoundland, you fool." she spat, pushing me away. "Don't you get it? The reason the Golden Plague was never stopped is *you*!"

"Don't you say that!"

"It's true! I could have *found* a cure in Newfoundland if you hadn't kidnapped me! I know it!"

The hairs rose on the back of my neck as I remembered what I'd once said.

We aren't arriving at pivotal moments in history. We're causing them.

"I thought I was doing the right thing," I whispered. "So did Alan."

"I know your reasons. I know *his* reasons." She swept waterlogged hair from her face. "And I don't care."

She turned her back on me and swam through the last barrier.

Three hours later, we reached New Hebrides. A group of Fishermen gathered as we emerged from the water and crawled, coughing and spluttering, onto the beach. A dozen willing hands pulled us to our feet.

"Where on earth did *you* come from?" One burly man pulled off my preserver. "Who *are* you?"

"My name is John Regulator Wayne," I rasped. "And I brought back a Goner."

I took the colt from its holster and threw it with all my strength into the sea.

"Now I'm going to see the Town Council."

By the time Florence and I approached the centre of the island, we had gathered quite a crowd. On the outskirts of the First Ring, we were halted by a Military unit. They seemed uncertain what to do with us.

"I want to talk to Douglas Judge Macarthur," I said loudly. "We have vital information for him."

"You're an exile, boy." A Sergeant strode up and twisted an arm behind my back. "You don't call the shots here."

"Get your damned hands off my son." I recognised the voice immediately.

It was dad.

He stepped out of the crowd and held up his badge. "I'll escort him to the town hall personally."

"Understandable." The Sergeant ordered his men to disperse the crowd. "We'll be watching."

"I never thought I'd see you again, boy." My father let the back of his hand brush mine as we walked. "How much trouble are you in this time?"

"Nothing I can't handle."

"Glad to hear it." His mouth twitched, trying to suppress a smile. "Your mother is going to be baking for the rest of the day when she finds out."

He turned to Florence, shivering beside me.

"And you are?"

"Still mad as all hell."

Douglas MacArthur met us on the steps, wearing his dark green robe and flanked by two similarly dressed judges.

"I'm somewhat speechless." He laced his fingers together. "Which is not normal for a public official."

"Who is the person with you?" A portly judge on the left stepped forwards.

Florence glared at him through wet, bedraggled locks.

"Tell him," I urged.

"Yes, woman. Speak."

"My name is *Mrs* Carver." She straightened up and squared her shoulders. "Mrs *Alan* Carver."

"We came from 2019," I added.

The fat judge looked like he might faint.

"Come inside." Macarthur recovered from the shock first. "Get dried and changed. Once you've rested, we can discuss this… turn of events."

"Thank you."

"Is there anything you'd like in the meantime?"

"There is," I replied.

"I'd like to see the historical records."

The records room was small and musty, holding only a desk, some battered plastic chairs and two computers. I sat at one, Florence hovering behind me like a vengeful ghost. She was still grieving and I doubted we would ever be friends again.

I typed in *Zac Rutter. Helicopter Pilot. New Hebrides. 2019.*

After a few seconds, a short entry came up. I moved aside so she could see properly.

Zac Pilot Rutter.

When the Carver Foundation was destroyed in the Great Chaos, Zac Rutter flew the last batch of DNA to the safety of New Hebrides. He also witnessed and reported the demise of the island's founder, Alan Carver.

Promoted to Captain, Rutter had a short but distinguished flying career, until he was well into his seventies. Unfortunately, his eyesight began to fail and he was informed he would soon be transferred to flight instructor duties. Sent on one last scouting mission, he refused orders to return to base and continued heading east until his plane was out of radio contact.

He was never heard from again.

"Alan never did like being told what to do." The woman squeezed my shoulder gently. "I'm going to work."

"I'm sorry, Florence."

"I know." Her voice was devoid of emotion. "You and my husband did what you had to and I'll eventually accept that. But I'll never see him again. You're going to be a constant reminder of that."

She smiled weakly.

"Y'know. *Being* him and all."

I hadn't thought of it in those terms.

"It'll be torture." She gave me a brief kiss on the head. "But I'll get over it in the end."

"I'm going home to have dinner with my parents." I pressed a key and the man who was really Alan Carver vanished into obscurity again. "From now on, I'll try and stay out of your way."

Mum smothered me in kisses and Dad shook my hand warmly but there was no disguising the tension between us. It didn't help that my new baby brother, Woodrow, was gurgling in the corner. The meal itself was spectacular, considering how few rations my mother had to work with, but I didn't have an appetite.

"Tell us about your adventures," Mum said.

I did. When I finished there was an astonished silence.

"I'd like to propose a toast." Dad finally poured himself a mug of potato hooch. "Would you join me, boy?"

"Robert, he's only fifteen!"

"He fought off a T-Rex with a catapult, Marie."

"I've already tasted wine," I added. "And coffee."

"To my son, John Wayne." Dad raised his drink. "The Saviour of New Hebrides."

Once I would have rejoiced at being given such a prestigious title. But it had come at too high a price.

"I don't like being called that," I said quietly. "Anyhow, nobody's supposed to know what I did. Not 'til Florence finds a cure. Apparently, she's only a few months away from doing so. Even less, now she has such advanced technology to play with."

"We're still proud." Mother nudged a brightly sprinkled coral cake in my direction. "We're also ashamed. Of ourselves."

"Mum?"

"We've never been as close as we might." Dad took a gulp of alcohol to fortify himself. "Maybe no father and son on this island does, not without real blood ties."

"Stop making excuses, Robert."

"I should have defended you properly," my father said humbly. "Tried harder to stop you being sent to the Towers or exiled."

"You would have been demoted or even banished." I forced myself to take a bite of cake. "Mum would have been left alone. You said so yourself."

"It was a tough decision, yes." Dad's hand trembled as he put down his glass. "I still called it wrong. You put me to shame."

"Don't ever say that. I've made a few similar tough decisions myself."

"Can't we put all that behind us?" My mother seemed to have aged years since I last saw her. "Be a family again?"

"It's a larger family than when I left." On cue, Woodrow gave a loud burp and Mum hurried to pick him up. "But I guess you can give the kid to someone else, now that I'm back."

I was joking, but my parents didn't see the funny side. I suppose some things never change.

"John!" Mum paled and clutched the infant tighter. "How could you say that?"

"We got him the same way we got you." Dad stood up and hugged his wife. "If I'm going to stand by my eldest son from now on, I have to stand by the youngest as well."

That was good enough for me.

"The Council want you to stay in isolation until a cure for the plague is found," he continued. "So nobody can ask you awkward questions."

He drained the mug.

"I'm not going to let that happen. This time, I don't care what it costs."

I looked at the three of them standing together. Realised they finally had a chance to start again and raise a son on the mainland. A son who wouldn't be turned into a thoughtless bully with a baton instead of a sense of right and wrong.

And what about Florence? It hurt her just to look at me.

"I *will* need your support," I said, avoiding Mom's eyes. "Because I have one more tough decision to make. This is what I have to tell the Town Council…"

Next day, Florence and I appeared in front of the High Councillor himself, old as the hills and resplendent in a white cotton robe. Judge James MacArthur was there at my request. So were Mum and Dad, wearing their Sunday best and almost radioactive with pride. Mum held my baby brother in the crook of one arm.

"I've inspected your labs, Sir." Florence glanced at her notes. "They're certainly sufficient for my purposes. I think I can isolate a strain of pesticide that will kill the wheat in less than a year.

When that's done, I should also be able to create a dimensional break within the Sixth Ring."

"What will that do?"

"It will stabilize New Hebrides in time. No more dinosaurs."

"Our scientists have assured me that's not possible."

"Your scientists couldn't build a gun mount that points anywhere but forwards," I pointed out.

"With all due respect, Sir." James MacArthur joined in. "They didn't design the Sixth Ring. *She* did."

"This is the answer to our prayers." The High Councillor gave a toothless smile. "Do you need anything else?"

"The statues of Alan Carver are wrong. He was better looking than that. Slimmer too."

"We'll put up a new one when we reclaim the mainland. Happy?"

"It's a start."

"As for you, young man." The High Councillor put on a pair of thick glasses and peered at me. "I think you deserve a reward."

"Thank you, Sir." I gave the Regulator salute. "In that case, I want you to banish me again."

Mum and Dad reached out and took each other's hands.

"I don't think you're getting the concept of *reward*." The official folded his arms. "Your father has insisted you live with them, so I'm prepared to give you a bigger house in the centre of the island. Until we can relocate to the mainland, that is."

He removed the glasses and cleaned them.

"It's got a fridge."

"That would be handy, now my parents have another son."

"Yes," the High Councillor said dryly. "Sorry about that."

"But I respectfully request permission to leave the island again."

"Request denied."

"John Wayne has a point, Sir." Judge McArthur tried to diffuse the situation. "He's a convicted Goner and we're supposed to have executed him."

"I hardly think that matters, given our new hope. Boy will be a hero, in fact."

"It will take Florence Nightingale up to a year to refine a cure for the Golden Plague." I clasped my hands together. "Give me that year. Let me head east again."

"You want to go round the world *twice*?" The High Councillor got up and walked stiffly round the desk. "Why would someone with everything to live for undertake such a risky enterprise?" He leered over me. "What did you find that was so important?"

"It's not what I found. It's who I lost."

"Ah. Now I understand." The High Councillor waved a shaky hand at Judge MacArthur.

"Permission granted. Give this child every resource he asks for."

I try not to take things too seriously. You never know what dangers life will throw your way, so why not live in the moment?

But those moments eventually become a past we will be judged on, even if it's only by ourselves. It's hard not to take *that* seriously.

I'd risked my life dozens of times to get back to this island. Achieved more than anyone could have expected. Once the Golden Plague was destroyed, I could bask in glory and be famous. Nobody would blame me if I decided to stay.

Yet, behind the excuses and the justifications we make for our actions, each of us truly knows what's right and wrong. Like John Wayne in those old movies.

I was right to leave my friends behind. If I hadn't, New Hebrides would have perished. But now Winston, Stan, George, Elvis and Jane were trapped between a past that wasn't theirs and a future already written.

Someone had to go back and rescue them. For once, I didn't need to think it through.

It would have to be me.

ABOUT THE AUTHOR

Jan-Andrew Henderson (J.A. Henderson) is the author of 40 teenage, YA, adult and non-fiction books. Published in the UK, USA, Canada, Australia and Europe, he has been shortlisted for fifteen literary awards and is the winner of the Doncaster Book Prize, the Aurealis Award and the Royal Mail Award.

www.janandrewhenderson.com